"AM I OVERDRESSED?"
SHE ASKED DEMURELY.

"In other circumstances I'd be anticipating removing what little you do have on."

Widening her eyes for effect, she replied, "You're too noble to even think such thoughts."

"Don't put me on a pedestal. I'm a man. If I weren't discriminating—" He stopped the thought.

Eyes narrowing, Elizabeth clenched her teeth. He'd put himself on a pedestal. So she wasn't good enough for El Exigente. By the end of the evening he'd know the reverse was true.

"Such chivalry!" she said, unable to control her sharp tongue.

"That was rather gauche. Pardon the slip."

Quickening her pace, Elizabeth lengthened her steps. With one long stride Jared moved ahead, pivoted, and stood blocking her path. Raising her chin with one curved finger, he said sincerely, "I'm sorry."

Faking a smile, she patted his cheek, thinking, *You're not nearly as sorry as you're going to be!*

A CANDLELIGHT ECSTASY ROMANCE ®

DESIGN FOR DESIRE

Anna Hudson

A CANDLELIGHT ECSTASY ROMANCE ®

Published by
Dell Publishing Co., Inc.
1 Dag Hammarskjold Plaza
New York, New York 10017

Dell ® TM 681510, Dell Publishing Co., Inc.

Candlelight Ecstasy Romance®, 1,203,540, is a registered
trademark of Dell Publishing Co., Inc.,
New York, New York.

ISBN: 0–440–11848–4

Printed in the United States of America
First printing—December 1983

To Hank, with love,
for being my candlelight lover,
who ecstasizes my life.

To Our Readers:

We have been delighted with your enthusiastic response to Candlelight Ecstasy Romances®, and we thank you for the interest you have shown in this exciting series.

In the upcoming months we will continue to present the distinctive sensuous love stories you have come to expect only from Ecstasy. We look forward to bringing you many more books from your favorite authors and also the very finest work from new authors of contemporary romantic fiction.

As always, we are striving to present the unique, absorbing love stories that you enjoy most—books that are more than ordinary romance.

Your suggestions and comments are always welcome. Please write to us at the address below.

Sincerely,

The Editors
Candlelight Romances
1 Dag Hammarskjold Plaza
New York, New York 10017

CHAPTER ONE

" 'Businessman seeking mistress. Age 21–35. Attractive. Intelligent. Write *Texas Star*, Houston, Texas.' Why don't you answer this ad?" Sara Hawkins asked impishly. "You'd make a dynamite mistress."

"You're doing it again," Elizabeth Sheffield softly but sternly answered.

"What?"

"Making me a victim of your fantasies. You dream up these compromising situations, then plop me in the middle of them." Elizabeth kept scanning the page she held between herself and Sara. "Answer it yourself," she suggested.

"I'm not qualified," Sara replied, patting her overly rounded stomach.

One-fourth of the newspaper fell forward as Elizabeth glanced at her blond-haired, blue-eyed,

11

slightly overweight friend. "Mistresses come in all packages and flavors. I believe the phrase men use is: All cats look gray in the dark."

Circling the ad with the red pencil she held, Sara cajoled her friend. "Come on, Elizabeth. Let's answer it. Just as a lark!"

Reaching over the coffee table, Elizabeth plucked the pencil from Sara's hands and snapped it in half. "You will not, I repeat, *not* respond to this ad. The last 'lark' you pulled almost had me singing the tune of a jailbird."

Giggling, Sara said, "But we did get to meet some handsome Houston cops. I still date Ryan."

"Setting off the burglar alarm in Dad's jewelry store and waving frantically in my direction is not my idea of how to meet men." Elizabeth snorted disdainfully.

"You were laughing harder than I was," Sara protested.

"Not until they took the handcuffs off." Sara's giggling was infectious. Melodically Elizabeth's laughter joined in.

"Seriously," Sara continued, a cheeky smile belying the word, "you're a twenty-five-year-old, well-stacked redhead, and smart as a whip. You satisfy all the requirements."

"Thanks, but no thanks. I'll struggle along designing jewelry, earning a humble but honest living."

"Ho-hum. Nine to five. Let's get some excitement into our lives." Sara's eyes were sparkling with enthusiasm.

12

"Why don't you embezzle some money from First National. That would put some excitement into *your* life instead of mine."

"Don't think I haven't thought of that. The only thing stopping me is Mr. Humbug Crosby, President of the No-Sense-of-Humor Club. But this," she said, pointing to the ad, "could be worth a week of chuckles. Doesn't it spark your curiosity?"

Snapping the paper back into its original upright position, Elizabeth replied emphatically, "No."

Having Sara around would try the patience of a saint, Elizabeth thought. Trite, but true. None of the employees at First National would believe their head teller was an overgrown child. *If impetuosity and mischievousness were qualifications listed in the ad, I'd send in Sara's résumé,* Elizabeth fumed silently. *Why not? Let her squirm in her own juice for a change.* Dark eyes gleamed; lips quirked upward. "Sara, babe. The fat is about to hit the fire . . . literally," she mouthed behind the newspaper.

The telephone interrupted the vision she had of Sara sputtering her way through an interview with the mysterious mistress-seeker.

"Hi, Dad," Elizabeth responded to her father's greeting on the phone.

"Want to play hostess? Free dinner at Nino's," he said, tempting her palate and pocket.

"Who's the client?"

"Tweedledum and Tweedledee."

Years ago, as a teenager, Elizabeth had bestowed Jim Hessel and Clayton Thomas with the nicknames that had stuck. They were two middle-aged, lookalike men who often competed for their jewelry purchases.

"In that case, I'd love to go. How was your trip to Australia?"

"Interesting. Wait until you see the opals I bought. Fire, light, depth . . . a designer's dream," he hinted.

"Care to sell some? Just remember my motto: Cheap is too expensive; nothing is all I can afford." Occasionally Elizabeth accepted a consignment from her father, but generally she preferred independent contracting. Independence and a strong father–daughter relationship didn't mix. Her creativity was apt to be stifled, as fatherly concern, smothered in tradition, did not mix with her contemporary designs.

George laughed at his daughter's favorite negotiating statement. Every bargain they made began with the same one-liner. "If Jim and Clayton buy, I'll deduct your commission from the cost of any opals you buy. Fair?"

"You just made a deal, Mr. Sheffield."

"I'll pick you up at six tomorrow. How's business?"

"Thriving. I'm checking the newspaper now for any manufacturers' advertising for craftsmen. Any company advertising for craftsmen needs designers also. By next week I'll have finished the designs for Silver Craft."

"Busy lady. Oh, incidentally, the sea gulls you designed for Carson are in the Sakowitz stores. Did he push for mass production?"

"Dad"—a warning note entered her voice—"you know how I feel about every woman wearing the same design. Carson knows I'll only contract for limited editions."

"Contrary to the success theories of Henry Ford, you're making a name for yourself in the industry. I'm surprised Carson didn't try to tempt those stubborn ideals with long, green cash."

"Unlike *some* people, he's given up."

"Don't get riled. If I didn't heckle you every now and then, you'd think I didn't love you," he said warmly. A clicking noise came over the line. "Sorry, love. I've got a call on the other line. See you Saturday. 'Bye."

"'Bye."

Replacing the phone on the cradle, Elizabeth yawned and stretched. Neatly folding the paper, she gracefully arose from the off-white sofa and began the nightly ritual of straightening the living room.

"Is that a hint it's time for me to go next door? Not very subtle," Sara rebuked, tucking the want-ads she had been reading under her arm. "Mind if I borrow these? One of the secretaries at work has a snowbird flying in from up north. There are a couple of good opportunities on the back page."

"You are not leaving here with that mistress

15

ad, Sara Hawkins. Tell your 'friend' to go to an employment agency, but leave my paper here."

The grimace on Sara's face reflected a plot being foiled.

"You have no faith . . ." Sara began.

"My dear, I have all the faith in the world that you'll set me up. Not this time."

"Opportunity is knocking and *you* are deaf." Tossing the want-ad section on the table, Sara stood up, pulling her shorts into place over her ample buttocks. "All work and no play . . ." She left the truism dangling.

"Makes Elizabeth independent and self-sufficient. A state of being I find immensely satisfying."

"Makes my vicarious experiences dull," Sara complained, shaking her springy blond curls vigorously. "If I had your face and figure, I'd have my résumé in the mail first thing in the morning."

"He's probably King Kong's twin. Forget it," she replied in dismissive tones that hid her own devious intentions. "How about going to the beach Sunday. You can watch male bodies at the South Jetty."

"Wear your turquoise bikini and I'll go."

One reddish eyebrow quirked upward.

"Ever wonder why 'Cellulite Sara' sticks by your side? You're the bait; I'm the trap," she teased, walking to the door.

"Don't pull that I'm-so-homely-and-you're-so-beautiful routine. Your dance card is full. Mine is empty. Care to explain that phenomenon?"

16

"Simple. You are a romantic waiting for Prince Charming to gallop into your living room. I date the beasts waiting to become princes. In other words, ole buddy . . . you're too picky."

"Well, Briar Rose, this picky princess is sleepy. My chaste bed is calling." Gently nudging Sara out the condo door, she added, "I'd feel sorry for you if I didn't know better. You've been engaged twice. I get propositions, not proposals."

Sara didn't reply. Cutting through the bushes separating their adjoining living accommodations, she hummed, "I'm Just a Girl Who Can't Say No."

Closing the door, Elizabeth headed into the bedroom, flicking off the lights as she went. Yawning, she stretched tanned arms high above her head, sluggishly moving into the bathroom. Scanning the glowing, healthy skin reflected in the mirror, she thought about Sara's parting remark. Picky. Was she too picky? Hadn't she dated a multitude of men as she searched for Mr. Right? Unfortunately she could categorize them neatly. Category One, labeled Hair and Teeth, held the men interested in a one-night-stand with a woman . . . any woman with her own hair and teeth. Category Two, labeled Air Heads, held the men scared to death of a woman with something more substantial between her ears than air. There were other men with redeeming qualities, she was certain, but where?

Opening a creamy face cleanser, she tilted the container and watched the pink lotion make a small, aromatic puddle in her palm. Using her fingertips, she applied the lotion to her wide brow, high cheekbones, curve of chin, thin upper lip, and fuller lower lip. The sweet fragrance intensified as the lotion crossed the bridge of her slightly uptilted nose. Following the same path, she removed it with a cotton pad.

Maybe I ought to put an ad in the paper, she mused. *"Wanted: Beauty seeking Beast who will eventually become Prince." Every weirdo in Houston would send a résumé.*

"A cynic at twenty-five." She spoke aloud to her reflection.

"I will *not* compromise," Elizabeth answered herself firmly. "Having a multitude of dates is like having a multitude of mass-produced jewelry—no quality in the whole bunch."

Sara's jibe about being too picky had really nettled her. Was she being childish; was she waiting for a prince on a white charger? In the mirror her artist's eye envisioned the mythical unicorn carrying a tall, dark prince into her waiting arms.

"The unicorn," she said, dark eyes twinkling. Dropping the brush she'd been using, Elizabeth rushed into the bedroom and picked up the pad and pencil by the side of her bed. Ten minutes later the fairy tale beast was winking broadly at her from the scratch pad. She could almost hear it saying "Believe in me."

Opening the door, Elizabeth embraced the tall,

silver-haired, impeccably dressed man who was her father, and ushered him into the living room.

"Do you have time for your favorite Texas margarita?" she asked graciously.

George flashed a warm smile, but shook his head. "Sorry. We have to be on our way." Pulling a jeweler's case from his pocket, he lifted the lid on the dark-blue leather case. Removing the contents from the white satin interior, he displayed the sparkling diamonds intricately surrounding fiery opals.

"Oh, Dad, they are beautiful," Elizabeth exclaimed. "Are these the new Australian opals?" She carefully examined the workmanship with a practised eye.

"Yes," he answered thoughtfully. "You don't think the opals overwhelm the diamonds, do you?"

Elizabeth tactfully answered, "You won't have any trouble selling this little trinket." Mentally she envisioned the opals in a plain setting that complimented their own brilliance. No glitter. A simple, elegant setting would suit her preferences.

Placing the necklace around her slender neck, George murmured, "The jewels' beauty is surpassed only by the beauty of the wearer."

She remembered hearing the same words being said to her deceased mother. Softly Elizabeth kissed his closely shaven cheek, saying, "Thanks, Dad."

"You're even as tactful as she was," he responded with a merry twinkle in his eye. She hadn't fooled him with her comment about the jewels.

"Before we get into one of those long-haired versus short-haired discussions, I suggest we head for the restaurant. You're too stubborn to change the designs anyway, and you know it."

"Stubborn, eh? Funny, I've always thought you had a monopoly on that quality," he teased.

"No, Dad. You're the original; I'm the copy," she rejoined.

"Good thing *you* couldn't be mass-produced. I'd be bald-headed, instead of gray-headed." Swatting her rear end playfully, he teased further. "If I make a sale tonight, my taste in jewelry will once again be vindicated by the superb taste of my clients."

"Ah-ha. You're proving my point again. These are original designs, not a copy of a copy of a copy." Elizabeth giggled childishly as she scampered through the open apartment door.

Traveling in his luxurious Lincoln, Elizabeth enjoyed listening to the anecdotes her father spun about his recent trip. As the car pulled in front of Nino's Italian Restaurant and stopped, she allowed a parking attendant to help her from the car. As they entered the restaurant, the odor of finely prepared food permeated the air, making Elizabeth ravenously hungry. A tall, dark-haired hostess checked the seating chart and led them through the china- and crystal-laden tables.

Definitely not a burger-doodle, Elizabeth thought

silently as she glanced up at the ledge overhead that held various antiques. The old-fashioned spaghetti-maker, spinning wheel, dolls, and other various keepsakes were artfully displayed.

Jim Hessel and Clayton Thomas were both standing as the Sheffields approached. Both men greeted Elizabeth with an "air kiss" and shook George's hand.

"You old dog," Jim said. "How could such an exquisite woman have anything in common with you?"

"Maybe it's the jewels she's wearing," George replied as he grinned and winked at his daughter. "You know how these young fillies clamor for older men who can shower them with diamonds." George seated his daughter, then all three men pulled the ornately carved chairs out and seated themselves.

"Chianti?" the wine steward asked.

Jim and Clayton were intently eyeing the necklace rather than the cleavage exposed by the strapless ivory gown. Neither heard the steward's question.

"Chianti?" he politely asked again.

"By all means," George answered.

Winking, Elizabeth acknowledged the twinkle of amusement in George's eyes. Their guests were bedazzled. George had a sale.

"Ah, youth," Tweedledee sighed. "That steward could make an alcoholic out of a prohibitionist." Jim tried to give the illusion of having heard the steward. No businessman wants to appear

21

overeager. "How about me using some persuasive powers on you, little darlin'." A devilish grin accompanied his words. One finger twirled an imaginary handlebar moustache.

Batting her eyes dramatically in a flirtatious southern-belle manner, and using her most affected southern drawl, Elizabeth replied, "Why, Jim, ah do declare, you're trying to steal my"—she stroked the opals— "heart."

"Jim, any offer you make, I'd gladly double for such a treasure," Clayton said, joining the verbal game.

Both men had played a similar game on many occasions. It had become standard routine to comment on the jewelry with the teasing hints of complimenting Elizabeth.

Clayton leaned over the table to touch the necklace. Staying the questing hand, George said with mock ferocity, "Look, but don't touch."

"I'm certain we could agree on something mutually beneficial," Clayton negotiated.

"Don't leave me out of this," Jim interrupted. "Couldn't all three of us work out an arrangement?"

"Elizabeth, I'd be interested in seeing what you can do for me," Clayton said.

Glancing at her father, she said saucily, "I'd love to have the opportunity to work for you." Reaching into her small evening bag, she pulled out a business card. "Give me a call anytime."

Groaning, George placed his hand over his daughter's. "I pay for the meal and you drum up customers." Rolling his eyes toward the ceiling, he said, "I teach her everything she knows and this is the gratitude I get."

Their game ended as they placed their dinner order. A low hum of voices could be heard coming from the draped booth adjacent to their table.

Lovers often occupied that seating. Privacy was assured when the deep maroon drapes were drawn. Surprised, Elizabeth noticed the drapes were open. A flickering candle was adequate for visual enjoyment of the cuisine, but did not provide enough illumination to allow her a glimpse of the occupants. Although she faced her dinner guests and appeared interested in their discussion about the Astros and the Oilers, she began tuning in to the conversations around their table.

Within minutes dinner arrived. Fettuccini Alfredo, smooth and creamy, served with veal picante, thinly sliced and lightly flavored with lemon and garlic. The side order of tortellini, pasta stuffed with ground meat and spices smothered in a white Italian sauce, was wickedly delicious.

George, Clayton, and Jim were enjoying not only the spicy food, but also an animated discussion of the upcoming elections.

Unintentionally Elizabeth began listening to the nonpolitical discussion taking place in the adjacent booth. Ears perked up as she heard "hiring" and "employment" enter the conversation.

"I feel guilty," a deep baritone voice said, "about the split between you and Steve, but, damn it, I can't hire someone to take your place." His voice became harsh and brittle. "Some vapid floozie, like the one over there, would apply for the job. My day would be spent protecting my billfold."

Elizabeth glanced at the table directly in front of the booth. A young, attractive, bleach-blonde, dressed elegantly in green chiffon, dripping with emeralds, was attentively listening to her distinguished dinner companion.

She wished she could see into the darkened booth to get a peek at the man who obviously thought he was God's gift to impoverished women.

"Not all women are interested in just your money," she heard a soft voice reply.

"It's my body?" he asked cynically.

Only when that bald spot is covered with hundred-dollar bills.

Her attention was momentarily diverted when Jim asked for the parmesan cheese. Bestowing him a warm smile, she handed the requested item across the table.

"Watch her smile at that old coot," the deep voice commented.

Once again Elizabeth turned slightly to see the object of their conversation. Blondie smiled from ear to ear.

"You're not the only one who can spot a gold digger. I'll personally scan all résumés," the feminine voice stated.

Deep male laughter came from the recessed

enclosure. "Even you couldn't stop a conniver like that. She'd rip you to pieces."

Arrogant male.

"Did you hear those men practically bidding on her? I'll bet she earned every diamond she's wearing."

Twisting, Elizabeth stared at Blondie's emeralds and male companion. Touching the diamonds at her throat, Elizabeth flushed. *That swine is talking about me!* Squirming in her seat, she contemplated spreading tortellini vigorously over the offender's head.

The wiggling attracted George's attention. Solicitously he inquired if everything was satisfactory.

"Fine, Dad," she answered, stressing the last word.

"Sugar daddy," the male voice uttered, disgusted.

"Are you sure you're okay?" Placing a cool hand on her cheek, George tested for a temperature. "Do you need to go home to bed?"

"Did you hear him offer to take her to bed right in front of those other men?" she overheard.

Unable to control her eyes, she flashed death daggers at the offensive voice.

"Oh, dear," the feminine counterpart said, "do you think she heard you?"

"No. She's probably looking for a higher bid."

Excusing herself, Elizabeth once again seriously considered inflicting bodily harm on the uncouth man, but opted for the powder room.

25

A conniving gold digger, she fumed silently, stomping to the lavatory. *I've fought male gold diggers all my life. That arrogant, conceited fool!* A growl came from the back of her throat. She tapped her foot in frustration. He's probably ugly, ugly, ugly. With warts, she added. Then, for good measure, with hairs hanging out of the warts.

She giggled at the mental picture of a bald man, hiding hairy warts with hundred-dollar bills.

Splashing her wrists with cold water, she planned her strategy. *If he thought I was a gold digger before, wait until he sees me in action,* she thought. *I'll paw all over Dad. I'll regale him with how women appreciate men who can afford them. I'll tell them women will do ANYTHING for the right price.*

Fluffing out her long, fiery-red hair, she prepared for battle. Mischievously, she lowered one eyelid at her reflection before departing for the battlefield.

As she weaved her way through the dining room, the light in her brown eyes dimmed. The back of a tall, raven-haired, broad-shouldered man, with a dark-haired, well-dressed woman, was all the dimly lit room afforded of the couple leaving the booth.

Feeling much like a leaky balloon, she watched the departing couple. *Damn. Damn. Triple damn. He probably doesn't have even one wart!*

The remainder of the evening was flat for Elizabeth. Diplomatically George suggested Jim and Clayton see the rest of the opal-and-diamond creations before buying. They agreed. Having

26

completed their dinner and their business, each of the three men shook hands. As George paid the bill, Clayton joked about the price of dinner being added to the cost of their jewelry purchases. Congenially the group parted at the door.

Elizabeth sighed as she slid into the Lincoln. After pounding the pavement all week, it was nice being pampered. She closed her eyes and relaxed. Job-hunting pressures were far in the back of her mind. Temporarily locked away.

Recalling being the brunt of the dark couple's discussion steamed Elizabeth. That arrogant fool, she thought. Men! They have free license to misconstrue every movement a woman makes. Couldn't that miserable species of the male sex see any family resemblance? Elizabeth reconsidered. There really wasn't much physical resemblance. She was a young version of her mother, except for the tiny earlobes that were similar to her father's. Elizabeth smiled. She could hardly expect the dark-haired stranger to identify her parentage that way.

He's still a brute. "Sugar daddy!" Blondie may have had a sugar daddy, but she certainly didn't. Her goals in life included marriage and a family— not being a rich man's toy. George's clients generally were kind, thoughtful, and courteous dinner companions. No more. No less. Certainly not lovers!

That cad must have thought I'd have a busy night with three lovers. "Highest bidder," Elizabeth snorted quietly. Couldn't that jerk see that they were interested in the jewelry? She glanced down. The bottom opal hung in the shadows of creamy breasts. Did he think their obvious stares were directed to her bosom? She silently laughed. How wrong the stranger was. Tweedledee and Tweedledum probably hadn't even noticed the cut of her gown.

In honest reflection she admitted to being dead wrong about his appearance. The stranger's height and muscular frame were impressive. Pity, she thought. He should have scads of warts for all the ugly comments he made about women in general, and herself in particular.

After thinking about it, Elizabeth's sense of humor made her chuckle to herself. They both were drastically mistaken. Would this cure her of eavesdropping? Not likely.

When they reached the door, George asked, "What is your agenda for this week?"

"I'm working on a new portfolio. A children's line." Unclasping the necklace, she handed it to her father.

"Don't be a stranger," he stated, placing the jewels in his suit pocket.

Lips tilted upward, she teased, "Wouldn't it better for your business if I were? With a little effort I could steal Jim and Clayton away from you."

"Competition doesn't frighten me." His voice lowered. "I'm proud of your success."

She smiled, stifling a yawn, then kissed his

cheek. Inserting the key, George opened the door.

"Night, Dad. Love you."

After the door closed, she heard her father check the doorknob, making certain she had locked it. Slipping off her strappy heels, she noticed a piece of bank stationery that had been tucked under the door.

> Elizabeth:
> Gems Unlimited is hiring. Heard it through the grapevine at work. If they are expanding their lines, they could be interested in *Monique.*
>
> Sara

Thoughtfully she fingered the message. Gems Unlimited might be interested in the new children's line. It would certainly be worth the price of a phone call to find out.

Shortly thereafter, Elizabeth slipped between sweet-smelling sheets and fell into a dream-filled world. Her lips curved upward as a tall, raven-haired stranger mounted on a white unicorn, covered with tortellini and wine, galloped through the streets of Houston.

CHAPTER TWO

"Ms. Sheffield, please be seated," a velvet-smooth southern drawl requested.

Elizabeth was delighted with the old-world courtesy of standing when a lady entered. In most offices this polite mannerism was omitted. Smiling broadly, she gracefully crossed the short span between them and sat in the chair provided.

What a hunk, Elizabeth thought silently. Jared McKnight, president of Gems Unlimited, was as refined and polished as the most precious of gems. The color of his eyes reminded Elizabeth of priceless jade.

"My card," she said brightly, extending the engraved linen pasteboard across the walnut desk.

Reading as he seated himself, "For the unique . . . BUY MONIQUE." The card snapped as he placed it on a stack of résumés. "A business card?

The mark of a true professional?" Jared McKnight asked in a controlled tone.

"Unfortunately too many women in my field don't take the profession seriously." Thoughtfully she added, "Free-lancing generally leads to part-time rather than full-time employment."

"I gather you are interested in full-time employment?" he asked, eyes narrowing.

"Definitely. This is how I support myself. And working for several employers is hectic. Especially when they all want my services at the same time. Creative juices don't flow nonstop." Elizabeth knew she was rattling but couldn't seem to stop the fast flow of words. This was a good account. Designing jewelry for Jared McKnight's company would be a real feather in her cap.

Green eyes flecked with gold swept from her golden-red chignon down the length of her slender neck, then deeper to the V-neck of her burgundy suit. Index finger at the side of his dark, lean cheek, his remaining fingers rubbed his smoothly shaven chin. The piercing gaze made her uncomfortable. Cows about to be auctioned were appraised in the same manner. Perhaps he wasn't as gallant as she had thought. So much for first impressions.

Stiffening her back, thrusting her chin forward, she suggested, "Perhaps my portfolio will give you a more accurate appraisal of my ability."

"Pictures?"

"Precisely." Elizabeth bent forward to retrieve the sketches she had made for the children's line

31

and the brochures displaying her designs that she had accumulated.

"I'd rather not, if you don't mind," Jared replied, stopping her movement. "Your wares are already attractively displayed."

Elizabeth fingered the three-dimensional gold boot in the lapel of her jacket. He certainly had excellent eyesight. "If you'd like to see it up closer, I'll take it off . . ." The detail work made the piece exquisite. Being in the business, he would appreciate the craftsmanship.

"That isn't necessary either," he replied hastily. The red stain creeping up from under his white collar deepened the color of his tan.

What kind of interview is this? Elizabeth thought. *He doesn't want to see my portfolio or examine the jewelry.* It was certainly going to be difficult to sell him on any ideas if he refused to cooperate.

"Do you mind my asking you a personal question?"

Elizabeth smiled. "Within the boundaries of propriety . . . fire away."

"Why *Monique*?"

"That's easy. Elizabeth is Victorian and doesn't project the image I prefer."

Jared nodded his head, accepting the explanation. "Why aren't you in the suburbs with a husband and babies instead of—"

"Mr. McKnight!" she interrupted sweetly. "Your male chauvinism is showing. Women in the twentieth century have many options. Besides, combining my career, demanding as it is, with being a homemaker wouldn't work for me; I'd become second-rate in both of them."

"Well," he chuckled, "a husband certainly would have to be super-understanding to allow you to continue working."

"Many men are," she responded curtly.

Long fingers extracted a buff-colored résumé from the stack at the side of his desk. Paper-clipped to the top was a small ad. Carelessly he tossed it over the width of the desk.

"What are you waiting for—a rich old geezer to buy all your time? Mercenary bitch, aren't you?" he asked with contempt.

The unwarranted attack stunned Elizabeth. What was his problem? Did he resent career women to the point of being abusive?

Oh, my God. She did it, Elizabeth thought, silently recognizing the mistress ad. *Damn you, Sara Hawkins!* Jared McKnight didn't want her to design jewelry. He wanted . . . Elizabeth's dark eyes shot sparks of indignation toward the handsome man confronting her. A thought simmered in the back of her mind. Jared McKnight and Sara Hawkins both needed separate, but no less memorable lessons. Stringing along this handsome brute in front of her practical-joking friend would teach Sara not to interfere in her life. Cutting and whittling on the ego of the owner of Gems Unlimited would be a pleasure.

Grimacing, Jared shoved the padded swivel chair away from his desk. "If I hadn't recognized your picture, you wouldn't be here." One hand ruffled through his hair as he moved around the desk and sat on the corner.

"Recognized me?" Elizabeth asked bewildered. "Have we done business together before?" Frantically she tried to remember selling any creations to his company.

"From Nino's. I saw you there with three men old enough to be your father," he said with scorn. "They were bidding on your . . . virtue."

"You were the man in the booth?"

"Correct." Their eyes locked in silent combat. Hard green shimmered over dark brown. Neither Elizabeth nor Jared blinked.

Intuitively she asked, "You didn't place the ad, did you?"

"Correct again. My sister's warped sense of humor altered my ad for a social secretary. She feels my demands on her off-hours destroyed her marriage and . . ."

Elizabeth watched as he halted the confidences he was verbally expressing. A mask of indifference shielded the vulnerability he had inadvertently exposed.

"I don't pay for sex," he stated, picking up the ad and ripping it in half. "But, in your case, I might reconsider. You are a tempting morsel, but unfortunately for you I'm unaccustomed to standing in line."

Crude, rude, and socially unacceptable, she fumed while covering her thoughts with what she hoped was a sexy smile. Her mind raced ahead of her mouth.

If he were really disgusted with the thought of hiring a mistress, why did he set up this appointment? Berating a stranger wasn't enough of a reason. Did he—

"Would you consider the position I had in mind before Mary altered my ad?" Jared asked, putting an end to her speculations.

"Why would you want a"—Elizabeth searched her vocabulary for a polite word describing the world's oldest profession—"soiled dove?"

A broad, tilted grin erased the disgust and contempt from his face. Tiny laugh lines appeared.

"Suspicions confirmed. Your name isn't the only thing Victorian about you. 'Soiled dove,' " he quoted, chuckling in amusement. "That is Dickens's terminology, for certain."

"Did you expect coarseness from a woman who very carefully chose her profession?"

"No. I expected . . . I hoped . . . I *suspected* the aura of innocence surrounding you wasn't false. Was I deceived? Are you beyond accepting a helping hand?" His voice held a gentle quality she ignored.

If he hadn't been the man in the booth, Elizabeth might had seen or heard the change. But all Elizabeth saw was red. On two occasions he had deemed her a woman of ill-repute. He obviously believed in the double standard: good women and bad women. Being slotted in the last category twice meant one of two things. He desired a "bad" woman, or he was a reformer. It would be interesting to find out which slot he fit into.

Adopting a sultry tone, she asked seductively, "I've been helped by a lot of men's hands, Mr. McKnight. Do you think I could work for you without the thought of having me in your bed running around in the back of your mind?"

A hard gleam entered his jade eyes. The crinkles around his eyes vanished. "I believe I made myself explicitly clear about standing in line. Your abundant experience leaves me cold."

Had he slapped her face and thrown down the gauntlet, her femininity couldn't have been more challenged. *Why you self-righteous prig! Do-gooder! Holier than thou!* Elizabeth forgot about Sara. All she could see was the tall, handsome man in front of her proclaiming to be immune to any advances she might make.

The possible satisfaction of accomplishing her original goal, that of getting a designing contract, while teaching Mr. Jared McKnight a lesson in self-control tickled her funny bone. Hadn't he tried to play God and manipulate her life? Doing a little manipulating of her own would be suitable revenge for the repeated slurs he'd made.

"Actually, Jared, I've always had this dream of designing jewelry." Purposely she widened and rounded her eyes. "I've read everything I could get my hands on about lapidation."

Jared covered his mouth, but couldn't keep deep laughter from rising from his chest. "You mean lapidaries. Lapidation is stoning someone to death."

"Oh," she responded, giggling. Elizabeth

knew the meaning of both words. Little did he know the substitution was in actuality a warning. "There are so many things you can teach me," she said, hoping her look was one of adulation.

"Do you have any drawings? I'd be happy to give you my opinion on your work."

"I don't have any with me," she lied, "but if you'd give me a chance, I'm certain I could live up to your expectations." Eagerness and breathiness blended into a convincing lie.

Jared glanced at his watch. "It's too late in the afternoon for you to get them and return here." Turning his calendar around, he quickly scanned the dated sheet. "However, I am free this evening. Perhaps we could get together over dinner and you could show me your drawings."

Again Elizabeth stifled a grin. Usually it was the man who suggested that the woman see his etchings. The contract she coveted was all but signed.

"I'd love it. You're so kind. I just don't know what I can do to show my appreciation."

"I'll think of something," slipped out of his mouth.

Elizabeth saw him flush at his automatic response. She knew he would have eaten those words with relish rather than have spoken them to her.

"Anything," she replied seductively, enjoying his temporary discomfort. "I'd be happy to meet you here or at the restaurant, if that is acceptable. I'd invite you to my apartment . . ." she dropped her voice and her head, hinting that she didn't want him to see where she lived. That was true. She didn't.

"Why don't you pick me up here," he said with kindness.

Playing her role to the hilt, Elizabeth arose and impetuously placed a quick kiss on his tanned cheek. A tiny electrical charge ignited as her lips grazed his softly scented skin.

As though he too had been burned, Jared jumped back.

"Sorry," she apologized. "I know you don't want to touch me," she said pathetically.

"No. No," he quickly denied. Taking a deep breath, he said, "You just surprised me with your spontaneity."

He was lying. He either felt the same spark she did, or was trying to control his baser instincts. Whatever, it was going to be fun watching him struggle with himself . . . and with her.

"Would seven o'clock be convenient?" he asked abruptly, changing the direction of the conversation.

"Fine." Picking up her portfolio, she headed toward the office door.

"Wear something appropriate for a champagne dinner," he instructed her.

"What are we celebrating?"

"The beginning of a new career for you," he replied, smiling.

"Until later," she said in a promising voice before swaying out the door.

A few minutes later Elizabeth sat in her car in

the parking lot, drumming her fingers on the steering column. Jared had fallen into her trap more easily than liquid gold spilling into a mold. Smiling smugly, she recapped her artful management of what could have been an embarrassing situation. *I'll have him eating out of my sullied fingers before the evening is over.*

Starting the engine, she plotted her strategy all the way home. Double entendres, subtle and not so subtle, raced through her mind, causing her to smile and laugh most of the way. There was something delightfully wicked about being thrown into a totally disreputable role.

Going past Sara's condo reminded her of how angry she'd been with her friend. Silently she reminded herself that she had considered sending Sara's application in. If the situation had turned out differently, she would probably still have been angry, but taking everything into consideration, she had to admit she was looking forward to the evening. Instead of stripping an inch of hide off Sara, Elizabeth was anxious to reveal how the interview had ended. Between the two of them they'd work up a conspiracy that would make Jared cringe from head to foot.

The phone was ringing as she opened the apartment door. Rushing across the living room, she picked up the receiver.

"Hello."

"Elizabeth. Thank goodness you're home. I've been calling every five minutes."

"Whatever for?"

"Well, I was worried about your interview. What happened?" she asked, wanting all the gory details.

"Nothing much," Elizabeth answered coolly, knowing the reply would drive Sara right up the wall.

Silence.

"I've been so worried. After I started thinking about it, I could picture you being robbed, raped, and pillaged," she said dramatically.

Again Elizabeth didn't respond.

"What happened," Sara demanded.

Laughing at Sara's overblown curiosity, Elizabeth decided she had meted out enough punishment. "Come straight home from work. You can help me get dressed for my opening performance in 'A Woman of the Streets.' " Gently placing the receiver down, she disconnected the line.

The phone began ringing immediately. Elizabeth laughed, knowing Sara would be bouncing around like a jack-in-the-box. Incessantly it kept ringing. She lifted the receiver and placed it on the table. Sara called her name over and over. Smiling at the agitation she was causing, Elizabeth strolled into her bedroom.

Flicking through the hangers, she eliminated most of her wardrobe as too conservative for the image she desired. Then, way in the back, she found a costume she had worn years ago to a college fraternity party. The bespangled red fabric, accented by long fringes in the front and back and mid-thigh slits on the side, had nearly cost her her virginity that night. Elizabeth walked out of the closet and draped the gown across the ivory coverlet on her bed.

"That should do the trick," she muttered. Laughing, she realized the double-meaning was particularly appropriate. Jared wasn't a college freshman eager to fulfill his sexual fantasies, but he wasn't old enough to be immune to the wide expanse of flesh exposed by the gown. At least she hoped he wasn't.

An hour later she had taken a leisurely bubble bath, washed and blow-dried her hair, and applied a generous amount of makeup. The heavy pounding on the door heralded Sara's arrival.

Eyes twinkling at the threats Sara was issuing through the locked door, Elizabeth took her time answering it. Subtle punishments were far more amusing than overt hostility.

"Why Sara," she said, faking surprise, "what are you doing here?"

"What the hell do you think I'm doing here." Angrily she huffed over to the phone, still off the hook, and slammed it onto the cradle. "Mr. No-Sense-of-Humor almost fired me when I called him *Mistress* Crosby. He thought I was making fun of his effeminate walk. You really got me in trouble."

Elizabeth lifted one eyebrow. "Why, my dear Sara. I wouldn't even consider doing anything that would endanger you or your reputation," she answered sweetly.

Sara had the grace to flush. Unable to keep a

straight face any longer, Elizabeth burst into a fit a giggles and hugged her distraught friend. Within minutes she revealed all that had happened at Gems Unlimited. Sara's eyes grew bigger and rounder as the story progressed, and she gasped audibly at various points.

"You're going out to dinner with him? Oooooh! I can hardly wait until you get home. That dress is perfect. I have the most outrageous pair of rhinestone earrings. You get dressed and I'll run and get them."

With the precision of a matador dressing before a bullfight or a knight regaling his armor, Elizabeth donned the slinky gown. Curves usually hidden by conservative suits were molded and accentuated. The plunging V-neck dropped within an inch of her navel, exposing the inner curve of her uptilted breasts. Four-inch fringes followed the same plunge.

A tiny white line between her breasts denoted the size of her skimpy bikini. Jared wouldn't notice the defect in the darkness, would he? Too bad she wasn't free-wheeling enough to sunbathe without a top.

Inhaling, thrusting her breasts forward, she moved closer to the full-length mirror. The twin globes swayed slightly; sexily accented by the swaying fringe. Pivoting, she checked the back view. The V plunged below the waist, suggestively pointing to her rounded derriere. The shimmering fabric cupped her bottom closely. The garment reeked of availablility.

Lifting the hem, she slipped spike heels on her narrow feet. Thin straps of red leather held the tall heels in place. Turning to the side, she bent one long slender leg forward. The slit opened, revealing the tanned inner thigh of her other leg. Not very subtle, she mused, but definitely provocative. Slender hips swayed erotically as she slinked out the door.

Sara was waiting in the living room with earrings dangling from her fingers. She grinned broadly at Elizabeth as she inspected her dress.

"Aren't these fantastic? I bought them at one of those snitzy places where they won't let you try them on. But you probably could have guessed that—look." Sara clipped one of them on and Elizabeth saw her problem. The last inch of stones rested on Sara's shoulder. "I guess my neck is too short. But they'll be perfect on you," she declared, wincing as she pulled the clip off her ear.

Moving to the mirror behind the bar, Elizabeth clipped them onto her small earlobe. They were the final touch to a completely outrageous costume.

"Wow!" Sara enthused. "I wish I could be a mouse in your pocket tonight. You really would make a fantastic mistress."

"I'm off to fight the Battle Against a Double Standard," Elizabeth quipped.

Driving back to the office building, she felt a twinge of conscience. Jared thought he was doing his boy scout good deed for the day, and she was

CHAPTER THREE

Elizabeth steered her sporty Mercedes into the no-parking zone in front of Jared's office building. Without switching off the ignition, she slid over to the passenger seat. One manicured nail pushed the button that automatically lowered the tinted glass. Thrusting her head out the window, she addressed the tall, lithe man leaning with casual grace against the aggregated exterior wall.

"Hey, big fella, wanna ride?"

Recognition and something else Elizabeth couldn't quite place crossed his features. Leaning back against the upholstered seat, she admired the coordinated ease of the man ambling across the sidewalk. Tanned hands gripped the chrome window encasement as he dropped to his haunches. His quick intake of breath indicated his reaction as his eyes swept down her neckline. As his head rose, Elizabeth saw golden flecks glowing brightly in his green eyes.

His well-shaped hand seemed unable to resist. It hovered over her collarbone. Knuckles dropped slowly, a millimeter away from tracing the edge of the fringe to the bottom of the enticing V. With each inch of descent, the nearness of his knuckles spread a delicious, unwanted warmth through her flesh.

"You certainly dressed for the occasion," he said with a husky drawl.

"Mr. McKnight," she said breathily, moving her lips to his ear, "you can touch. My profession isn't contagious."

The tanned skin over his knuckles whitened as Jared clenched his hand and extracted his arm from the car interior. The mask dropped in place and hid any facial reaction from her.

"Right," he tersely answered.

Elizabeth hadn't been able to resist reminding him that "do-gooders" don't fondle the evil person they are trying to save. He obviously hadn't wanted to touch used merchandise. *He will before the evening is over,* she promised herself.

Jackknifing his body erect, he strode from the sidewalk around the rear of the car. Opening the driver's door, he lowered his beautifully dressed frame into the seat. Without even looking at Elizabeth, he wheeled the car away from the curb.

"I brought some designs." She had taken sketches done early in her career and had replaced the ones in her portfolio with the less-professional drawings.

"I'm anxious to see them," he responded, glancing at the rounded curve halfway down the neckline.

Casually she allowed her long leg to move through the slit and bend toward him. Two of her fingers edged from his knee to his jacket. She came close to spoiling the effect by giggling when she felt his leg muscle tense as his jaw clenched.

"I hope they're good enough for you," she sighed.

"Woman, unless you want to be a highway statistic, I suggest you control yourself."

A smile of victory flickered over her face. Jared's eyes were hungrily feasting on her silk-clad leg. Primly she removed it from his line of vision by covering it with the floor-length shimmering cloth. Only a sliver of thigh remained visible.

Trailing her fingers back down to his knee, the involuntary effect she was having was apparent immediately by the bulge in his trousers.

"It's hard . . . controlling my natural urges. You are an attractive man, Jared." Just the right amount of wistfulness was in the statement.

Using his right hand, he removed her fingertips gently and twisted his suit jacket to the left. "I'm having difficulty with a few urges of my own," he admitted. "We'll work it out," he said with confidence.

Jared didn't realize the double meaning of his last sentence immediately. When he did, he glanced at Elizabeth to see which way she had taken it, and groaned.

Smiling like the proverbial Cheshire cat, she murmured, "I'll do my very best for you."

Signaling left, he entered the On ramp for highway 610.

"Where are we going?" she asked casually.

"I made reservations at the Houston Post Oaks."

"At the hotel?" Her voice nearly squeaked.

"In the dining room," he replied curtly, giving her a disparaging look.

"Darn," she teased. Reaching to the dashboard, she turned on the stereo. Kenny Rogers's love ballads filled the silence. Through lowered lashes she glanced at the silent driver. He had changed from the gray pinstriped business suit to a darker, solid gray suit. The color accented his deep tan and the brightness of his eyes. Momentarily she wished he hadn't mistakenly assumed the worst.

Dreamily she stared out the front windshield and listened to the gravelly voice singing words of love. Several tunes later, Jared pulled off the highway on to Westheimer. A horn beeped as he switched lanes. Automatically her hand clutched the padded dash.

"I'll take care of you," he said, flashing a smile. "Good employees are valuable."

Elizabeth could feel the contract in her purse. The one thing she had to make certain of was to continue playing the role he had relegated to her.

48

Later, much later, when he was pleased with her work, she would reveal the truth. Not until then.

Moments later the car was parked and he was helping her out of the front seat. Courtesy obviously demanded he touch her, but only in a gentlemanly way. Taking her hand, he placed it in the crook of his elbow. He inhaled deeply as he opened the door leading to the dining room. He had seen the deep V in the back of her dress.

"It's going to be tough protecting your front and your rear flanks," he said with an amused inflection in his voice.

Chuckling, Elizabeth returned her hand inside his elbow and rubbed her thigh against his provocatively. "I'm certain you're up to it. Am I overdressed?" she asked demurely.

"In other circumstances I'd be anticipating removing what little you do have on."

Widening her eyes for effect, she replied, "You're too noble to even think such thoughts."

"Don't put me on a pedestal. I'm a man. If I weren't discriminating—" He stopped the thought.

Eyes narrowing, Elizabeth clenched her teeth. He'd put himself up on a pedestal. So she wasn't good enough for El Exigente. By the end of the evening he'd know the reverse was true.

"Such chivalry!" she said, unable to control her sharp tongue.

"That was rather gauche. Pardon the slip."

Quickening her pace, Elizabeth lengthened her steps. With one long stride Jared moved ahead,

49

pivoted, and stood blocking her path. Raising her chin with one curved finger, he said sincerely, "I'm sorry."

Not nearly as sorry as you're going to be! Faking a smile, she patted his cheek. "I'm used to being mistreated. Occupational hazard. It hurt because I expected more from you." Her conscience struck again when she saw the guilty expression on his face. He hadn't meant to offend her. Just a bad case of hoof and mouth disease: walking and talking without thinking.

Stepping back to her side, he lightly touched her elbow, guiding her into the dining room. "I'm certain your occupation was forced on you."

Little do you know you're the one doing the forcing.

"I'd like for you to tell me about it if you can."

Elizabeth's mind began inventing a properly sad story. She could refuse to divulge the information, but it would be better to curry his favor by creating a pathetic sob story.

Seated at the table, he began coaxing the tale of woe from her.

"Were you poor?"

"Not exactly. There were things I wanted and couldn't have, but I wasn't poor." Elizabeth had decided to keep as close to the truth as possible. Lies were difficult to remember for someone basically truthful. The role was becoming more difficult with each probe.

"A runaway?"

"No," she answered quietly. She had to think

50

up one preposterous statement to end the questioning.

"Are you uncomfortable talking about it?" he asked with concern.

"No." *Hell, no. I'm just struggling to keep one step ahead of your questions.* Like the light coming on in a dark room, the answer popped in her head. Outrageous! Delightfully wickedly outrageous. A gleeful smile drew her lips upward. She'd let him use his imagination, then lay it on him.

"Did your father . . . abuse you?"

Appearing to misunderstand the question, she said, "Oh, no. My daddy loves me."

Jared's tan darkened. "You mean, he . . ."

Appearing to catch the drift of his meaning, Elizabeth clasped her hand over her mouth. "Jared! Dad doesn't completely approve of my line of work, but—" Thoughtfully she stopped. "Come to think of it. Some of his friends are my clients."

One finger raked around the inside of Jared's collar. *Sorry, Dad,* she apologized silently. A giggle escaped when she realized how truthful her statement was.

"I'm becoming decidedly uncomfortable. Twenty Questions are over. Tell me about it."

Elizabeth looked around the room, creating an air of secretiveness. Leaning toward him, she cupped her mouth and spoke directly into his ear.

"I am a nymphomaniac."

Those four words were better than dumping tortellini and wine over his head. The muscle in

51

his jaw was visibly jumping up and down as she softly kissed it.

"I told you this afternoon that I chose my profession. I like it. No, I love it." Her voice sank into creamy, velvet sultriness, "And frankly, my dear, I've got the hots for you."

Elizabeth contained a combination snort and giggle behind her hand. Jared had absolutely paled. He looked as though he was on the verge of running out of the restaurant like a frightened virgin. In a flash the distraught look was replaced by an unemotional mask.

"Have you sought professional help?"

"I've tried everything. There is only one remedy for the constant ache I feel." Lifting her eyes, she beseeched him, "Help me, Jared. The one time I forget about my problem is when I'm working on a sketch."

Seconds passed before Jared replied. *Now his mind is racing*, Elizabeth thought triumphantly. *Spin away baby! The end result will be the same after you've tied yourself into knots: A contract in my purse.*

"I don't know that I'm the person to help you, Elizabeth. It would be like putting the fox in with the chickens." A self-deprecating smile tilted the corners of his mouth. "Let me think about it over dinner."

Oops! I overplayed my hand. He hasn't even seen my designs.

"Perhaps if you could see some of my work, it would help you make a decision. If I don't have any talent, I won't be of any use to you."

"Do you feel as though men use you?"

Elizabeth sighed with exasperation. He was stuck on solving her imaginary problem, and she wanted to get on with business.

"May I suggest, before your amateur psychological analysis begins, that we eat dinner. I'm starved."

With one hand he motioned to the waiter.

"We won't need a menu," he said, dismissing the tall leather-bound menu. "We will have chateaubriand medium-rare, baked potato, and house dressing on the salad."

"Yes, sir," the waiter said with deferential courtesy.

Perversely Elizabeth considered countermanding the order. But starting an argument now would only give him an excuse not to offer her a job. Getting that contract was becoming more and more of a challenge.

"Thank you for ordering for me. You're such a gentleman," she complimented him insincerely.

"You're welcome. I didn't want you to feel uncomfortable with either the choices or the prices."

His consideration was making her spiteful thoughts stick in her craw. The complexity of the man was bewildering. When she thought he was being arrogant, in actuality he was being thoughtful. When she tried to give him halo-type attributes, he readily admitted to being a sinner. Elizabeth had the sneaking suspicion he wasn't going to be easily manipulated. Above all else, she knew she was going to have to keep the slurs he had made firmly in her mind, otherwise . . .

Both of them had slipped into their own private thoughts. When she glanced up, her dark eyes could see the mental gymnastics Jared was going through in an effort to solve the problem she had confronted him with. Brooding, he stared at an empty table nearby. Shrugging slightly, his eyes shifted to her face.

"Would you mind if I sent one of the busboys out to the car to get your portfolio? Now is as good a time as any for me to go through it."

"Good idea," she responded quickly.

A five-dollar tip later, they were leafing through the sketches. The first five were quickly glanced at and dismissed. They were amateurish. As Jared progressed toward the back of the folder, the pages slowed down perceptively.

"You're talented. No doubt about it," he enthused. "I could use several of these. This one," he said, pointing to the unicorn, "would be particularly appealing to young horse-lovers. Many of the girls are riding horses and reading fairy tales at the same time. Good Christmas item."

Elizabeth glowed. "I'd like to mount a stone for the eye, which would give the appearance of twinkling with devilry or winking at the owner."

"Hmm. Good idea. Have to be a semi-precious stone. I don't want the cost to be prohibitive for what I have in mind."

"Exactly what do you have in mind?" she inquired.

"Millions of these trinkets distributed around the nation," he answered thoughtfully, not looking up.

Elizabeth wadded the napkin in her lap. "Wouldn't it be nice to produce a limited edition? Make them a real treasure. Sort of the heirloom type of gift," she suggested, trying to talk him out of mass-producing her designs.

"Not as lucrative. The unicorn design could be used as a charm, locket, necklace, bracelet . . ." he said, ticking off the possibilities faster than a Geiger counter over a uranium deposit.

"But if you'd use fourteen karat gold, make it three-dimensional, and use a precious stone, it would be of greater value and you could charge more for it."

Taking a pen from his breast pocket, he began scribbling in the margin surrounding the drawing. "Let's see. If we mass-produce a hundred thousand of these, the profit would be approximately . . ." Jared finished by naming a large figure.

The calculations were made faster than Elizabeth could have with the aid of a computer. "Granted you can make a large profit on these trinkets, but it isn't what I had in mind at all." Professional ethics of her own making were rising to the surface. She could sell the sketch to any number of jewelry houses with punch-out machines. "I prefer something unique."

Green eyes rose from the notebook. "Rhyming with Monique?" he asked dryly. "You're in a different business now. Monique passed away the moment I opened this book."

The conversation was interrupted by the waiter serving their dinner. The timing was bad. Elizabeth had wanted the matter clarified immediately. The challenge of getting the contract fell short when her personal ideas on jewelry designing were being threatened.

"That's enough business for now," he said firmly, slicing the tender beef. "Let's enjoy our dinner and negotiate a deal later."

There was no point in arguing. The thought of her work dangling in every dime store in America sickened her. It was like asking a fashion designer to create a sweat shirt selling for under five dollars.

Gripping her knife, she carved the meat with a vengeance. "Where's my salad?" she demanded grumpily.

"The waiter started to bring it earlier, but I waved it away. We were right in the middle of discussing your sketches."

"Business comes before nourishment?" she asked, astounded at his high-handedness.

Elizabeth could almost hear him counting to ten before answering. Picking up a hot roll, he said quietly in a flat voice, "You placed your portfolio above sex. For a nymphomaniac, that places your work far above the need for food on your priority list. Do you want a salad now?"

"No," she huffed, stabbing a piece of meat on the tongs of her fork.

"Is there anything you would like?" he asked politely.

Elizabeth's eyes glared at him. *I'd like to pick my baked potato up and grind it into your face,* she thought furiously.

"Don't," he warned as if reading her mind. "I don't want a scene."

"You're too much of a gentleman to cause a scene," she jibed.

"An acquired trait," he stated succinctly.

"You mean you weren't born with a mass-produced, stamp-out silver spoon in your mouth?" she asked sarcastically.

"Lady, and I use the term lightly, I've scratched for everything I've acquired. There have been times in my life when the rattle of silver in my pocket would have been the sweetest of lullabies. A stranger gave my dad and me a chance and we took it. No stipulations. No negotiating. Nothing. Nothing but gratitude. Our problems weren't the same, but were equally severe. Now I'm going to give you a chance, and a warning: Don't mistake my offering a helping hand as stupidity or weakness on my part. You'd be flat-assed wrong. I've pussy-footed with you so far today and reacted the way you thought I should react. That's over. No two-bit—"

"Care to put your money where your mouth is mister?" Elizabeth asked coolly, stopping him before any other words could pass through his lips.

"You don't stand a chance. I was street-wise before you were born. What you thought was clever manipulation today was merely curiosity on my part. Don't be lulled into thinking I can be led anyplace I don't want to be led."

"Totally in control of your destiny, are you?"

"Right on."

"Never thrown off step."

"Marching to my own beat," he countered. "Now that we've dissected my character, let me tell you about yourself."

"Do tell," she replied in a superior fashion, expecting repudiation for being a high-class call girl.

"Elizabeth Sheffield, designer of Monique Jewelry. Known in the business as talented, creative, a veritable genius. Also known for her opinions on mass-produced jewelry. You're no more a nymphomaniac than I am a eunuch. But don't fret, Monique. I'll still abide by my hands-off policy." He smiled coldly.

A smirk was Elizabeth's only response to his quietly controlled tirade. "I may not be a 'soiled dove,' but I'll bet I could easily get you into my bed. You have about as much self-control as a rutting bull," she said disparagingly.

Jared halted any pretense of eating. Dropping his roll in the center of his plate, he asked, "What's your bet, woman?"

Elizabeth paused, formulating her thoughts.

She wanted an exclusive contract with his company. Silently she measured his weaknesses. The crack about his manhood was the closest she'd come to finding a weakness in the self-made millionaire sitting across the table. She felt a drop of perspiration roll from under her arm down the bareness of her side. Fleetingly she wondered if there was a ring under the arm of his crisp white shirt.

"Within a month I can have you crawling, begging to get into my bedroom," she said, matching his arrogance. "And if I do, I get to write the contract on my designs. If I don't . . . you get to write the contract."

"It's a bet."

"Not so eager, Mr. McKnight. I'm not foolish enough not to have clauses in the bet."

"Loading the dice?"

"Perceive it as you wish."

"Continue, by all means," he urged, a devilish smile making the crinkles beside his eyes appear.

Mentally she began plugging the obvious loopholes in the bet. The scales would be tipped in her favor from the beginning. No point in betting if you were in constant fear of losing.

"No other women," she negotiated.

"Agreed, with stipulations. First, no other men."

"I'll have no trouble controlling *my* urges, Jared."

"Second, for this to be any challenge at all, we have to spend the month together."

"What do you mean, together?" Elizabeth asked warily.

"I still need a social secretary. I have commitments that require an organizer and the presence of a hostess. Take the job for the month and you have a bet."

"Not so fast, buster. I have a few more conditions of my own."

"Shoot."

"No out-of-town trips unless I go along."

"Agreed."

"You'll provide work-space for further designs, and begin making the molds for the unicorn and anything else I come up with."

"Aren't you taking my capitulation for granted?" he asked in an amused voice.

"If I sound smug about the outcome, it's because I am," she tossed back. How could she lose when he was allowing her to make the rules? She couldn't!

"Are you finished loading the dice?" The amusement in his eyes traveled over his face, encompassing his lips, tilting them into a wide grin.

"One more point should tidily wrap up the package." Leaning toward him so no other ears could hear, she made the last stipulation sotto voce. "To put it crudely, should you get into my bedroom, I don't have to come across."

"Scared I might succeed?"

"Not unless you resorted to brute force," she whispered, raking one fingernail down the sandpaper texture of his face. "You'll lose."

"Not a chance. By December there will be unicorns in every discount store between Maine and California. And, my dear, you'll be the one doing the begging." Catching her hand before she could return it to her lap, he brushed his lips over her knuckles. The kiss sealed the bet.

Begging, in her book, came right before borrowing and stealing. *I won't beg,* she mused, confident of her feminine wiles. *Wouldn't it serve him right to end the evening on his knees?* Rubbing the short dark hairs on the back of his hand, her dark eyes gleamed with a devilish sparkle of intent. The gleam bounced back off the wicked gleam of green jade.

"Lost your appetite for food?" he asked with a hint of sexual arrogance. Turning his hand over, he appeared to be measuring the difference in the lengths of their fingertips.

"Normally beggars can't be choosers, but I'll be magnanimous and let you make the next move."

Jared gave a relaxed laugh as he traced her love line and gently kneaded the firm flesh beneath her thumb. "The gleam in your eyes is a dead giveaway, Elizabeth. What little deception is being hatched beneath those fiery tresses?" As the last lilting word was spoken he sipped the tip of her finger, as though it were a fine wine.

"Why, Jared, your deception was far more adroit than mine. There were several times today I thought you'd perish at the thought of touching me, much less being . . . intimate."

"A good businessman plays more roles than an actor. Fooling you was a piece of cake. You lack the sensuality of a round-heeled call girl." Jared winced as her fingertip raked his chin.

Lowering her eyes, Elizabeth returned the hand he had held to her lap. Was that true, or was he manipulating her again? Did he honestly believe she wasn't woman enough to seduce him? Or was the disparaging remark meant to make her lose control of her temper and spoil the possibility of seduction. Patting her lips with the napkin whose seam had unraveled during her contemplation, she decided to see what role he was playing and beat him at his own game.

"Shall we go upstairs and continue this discussion?" Jared suggested, signaling for the waiter to bring the check.

"Upstairs to the bedroom suites, or to Maribelle's?" she sweetly asked, practically tasting victory as she encouraged him to begin the begging.

"We'll begin at Maribelle's . . ." The dangling sentence was the carrot placed in front of the horse. *Are you woman enough to make me crawl on my knees to the bedroom?* his pause asked. Was his grin another slam at her sexuality, or a victorious smirk?

Music accompanied the swooshing sound of the opening elevator door. Elizabeth could see the four-piece band that provided the background for a willowy singer crooning a familiar love ballad. Walls of glass overlooked the Houston skyline. Lights from a nearby office building lit the outside darkness, competing with the stars twinkling in the distance.

As they were escorted to a small low table for two near the dark windows, Jared ordered champagne, and without either of them sitting first, asked Elizabeth to dance. The small parquet dance floor was crowded. They've never seen the romping and stomping of the Cotton-eyed Joe, Elizabeth thought when she felt herself turned and nestled in Jared's arms. Both his hands molded her to the length of his tall frame. Unbuttoning his jacket, Elizabeth sensuously moved her palms up the front of his pale silk shirt. The fleshy part of her fingertips traced his collar, outlining his neck before interlacing. As she massaged the short dark hairs at the nape of his neck, Jared tightened the embrace, making her aware of the effect her fingertips were having on his libido. Gently his knee nudged between her legs as they swayed and turned. The embrace became reminiscent of liquid gold being poured into and conforming to a mold.

"You're a beautiful, intoxicating witch," Jared said huskily into her ear. "Oh, that you *were* a nymphomaniac. We wouldn't be wasting time on a dance floor."

Stretching her arms back, Elizabeth raised her face upward. As her shoulders pulled away, her hips pressed closer. The eyes above her became the sleek color of highly polished jade. Slowly his hand circled her bare back.

"The dossier you recited earlier didn't include my sexual inclinations," she whispered only inches away from his lips. "Are you certain your source of information was thorough?" Swaying to the beat of the music, hips moving in unison, she teased, "Don't claim to be a eunuch . . . I know better now."

Long fingers pressed her back against his chest, flattening her breasts against his torso. "I've wanted to hold you all day. You were made for love." His warm breath feathered the hair at her temples before his lips, equally light, kissed the sensitive flesh.

The wine, the music, and the hardness of his body made the blood surge heatedly through her veins. She felt his hand stroke from under her hair down the bare skin to her spine. The possessive hold increased as his hand slipped inside the deep-fringed V, moving to her rib cage. Fingers teased the flesh scant inches from her taut breasts. The flames he had previously kindled with his knuckles caused her defenses to totally drop. She clung to him. The dance steps became a mere swaying.

His lips touched her brow, temple, and moved to her ear. She felt the dampness as his tongue traced the path leading to her earlobe, which he gently nipped before breathing shallowly into the shell-like orfice. Wantonly she responded by gently rotating her hips against him.

What would it be like to make love to Jared, she wondered. *He's definitely experienced. His finesse on the dance floor is proof positive of that. He'd make it a glorious experience.*

Her eyes closed, she imagined the feel of his chest against her without the restrictive clothing. Her fingertips itched with the desire to run them through the hair—dark, curly, thick, she knew was hidden beneath the silky fabric. Unconsciously her lips moved to the pulse beating at the point above his collar. Beneath his well-fitted suit jacket, she knew his arms and shoulders would be muscular and smooth to the touch, a contrast to the dark hair she would nuzzle while stroking them. Breathing deeply at the erotic thought, she inhaled a blend of soap and masculine aftershave. The tip of her tongue unerringly traced upward until she could no longer feel his blood pulsating through his veins.

A quick, sharp intake of breath near her ear dispelled the fantasy, and her dark, slumberous eyes opened. The image had been so clear in her mind, for a moment she was disoriented on the dance floor, and stepped on the edge of Jared's shoe.

"Sorry," she mumbled, glancing around the dance floor somewhat embarrassed by her wanton behavior. No one appeared interested in anyone other than their own partners. Spine stiffening, she realized Jared was seducing her on the dance floor.

"Let's go back to the table," she requested, loosening the slender arms wrapped around his neck.

"My barometer is climbing close to the hot and humid level," he whispered softly into her ear. "Aren't you interested in a quick victory?"

A rapid defeat was all Elizabeth envisioned. Jared knew every trick in the book listed under "Seduction on the Dance Floor," and he was effectively using his knowledge. Pliantly she had accepted his expertise without using any of her own. Silently she vowed, as she snuggled closer, to correct the error in strategy. He'd be the one leaving the floor breathing hot and heavy, and she'd be calm and cool.

Humming the ballad the instrumental group was playing, she intentionally let her lips vibrate against the pulse she had kissed earlier. Stretching on tiptoe, she circled the outer shell of his ear with one finger and said breathily, "Let me know when the barometer reads Explosion Imminent."

Parting her lips invitingly, she tilted her head back, eyes purposely heavy-lidded, and moistened the curve of her lower lip.

"Ah," Jared moaned, eyes locked on her mouth. "Seductively executed, lovely witch, but unnecessary. I wanted to kiss you hours ago."

"Why didn't you?" Elizabeth asked, their breath warmly mingling.

"Anticipation heightens the senses. Aren't you wondering what my kisses will be like?"

I've wondered about more than kisses, she answered silently, honestly. "Am I going to find out?" she baited.

The string of slow ballads drew to a close. Elizabeth eased away, glancing in the direction of the band. Would they begin playing again? The lead musician answered her question by announcing a ten-minute break.

I'll need every second of those minutes, she thought, *to prepare myself for the next onslaught.* His hand placed low on her naked back guiding her back to the cozy table for two was having the same effect as an electrically charged wire. Tingles swept up her spine, causing goose bumps on her arms. Involuntarily she shivered.

"Cold?" Jared asked, noting her shiver and rubbing his hand down her arm, over the hairs standing on end. "I can warm you up," he whispered huskily for her ears only. "Let's go."

"Would you mind my going to the powder room first?" she asked, needing to repair the emotional havoc he had wreaked on her nervous system more than she needed to repair her make-up.

Jared consented by nodding his head. "Don't bother applying any lipstick," he instructed with a devilish grin.

Elizabeth left the darkened room, weaving through the tables, bumping into one couple in her haste to get away. The rest room was small but plush. The rise in flow of adrenaline made her pace back and forth while she feverishly tried to bring herself under control.

"He's probably arranging for a room right now," she muttered to her reflection in the gold-framed mirror. A beige object on the wall behind her shoulder offered another possibility. "A phone! I'll call Sara and have her rescue me. Cowardly but convenient."

Pivoting on the ball of her foot, she crossed the short distance and lifted the receiver. No dial tone. Forcefully she slammed the receiver back on the hook. She'd left her purse at the table. No money. Every route of escape seemed blocked.

The door swung open and the night club's hostess walked in.

"There's one fine-looking gentleman out there. He asked me to come in and see if you're okay."

"Thanks, I'm fine now. Do you have a quarter?" The embarrassment of asking a stranger for money paled in her need to escape.

"Sorry, hon. My purse is locked up. Would you like for me to ask your friend for one?"

"No! I mean, no, thank you. Tell him I'll be right out."

Smiling, the hostess left.

"Get angry," she instructed herself. "He's arrogant, conceited, and . . . he tricked you." Her finger pointed at the mirror. "You're here to teach him a lesson, not be a willing pupil."

The short pep-talk put cold, hard steel in her spine and a straight-lipped purposefulness on her lips as she swung the door open.

Jared stood directly across from the door, his hand clasping her spangled purse. The incongruity of the virile man holding a dainty evening bag caused Elizabeth to cover her mouth to hide a wide grin.

Extending the purse in her direction, Jared said, "Not funny. Some smart aleck just asked to borrow my eye liner." Deep chuckles joined her own light laughter. "Come on, woman. Let's go to my place." Draping his arm over her shoulders, he pulled Elizabeth close to his side and headed toward the elevator.

As they entered the elevator she broke away from his light hold. Facing him, she looked straight into his eyes. "Jared, we need to talk about our bet," she implored.

"It's settled. You set the terms. I agreed to them. That's final." Jaw thrusting forward, he said the words as though a bad taste had entered his mouth.

Strong hands clasped the soft flesh of her upper arms as his lips came down to hers to stop any further haggling. The lips were hard as they twisted over hers, seeking entrance. Elizabeth struggled against him. Fists pushing against the lightweight fabric of his summer suit, she began to panic. Jared demanded a response, but the pressure eased. His lips began moving gently, sensuously, teasing the lower lip. The demand changed to longing. No man had ever kissed her with such longing. Wrapping her arms around his waist, she willingly parted her lips.

As he began to deepen the kiss, Elizabeth

heard a loud, "Parrrrdon meeeee!"

Instantly she started to pull away, but Jared drew her back into the protective shelter of his arms. She knew how the mating dogs on her front lawn had felt when her dad had thrown water on them. Cheeks flaming at the thought, she ducked her head into his shoulder, away from their audience.

"Honeymooners?" the stranger asked, chuckling.

"Yes," Jared replied succinctly, hustling her out of the elevator into the corridor.

Elizabeth was shocked by his reaction as she felt his chest begin to rumble with restrained laughter. What, in a totally embarrassing situation, tickled his funny bone?

"I haven't been caught necking in an elevator in fifteen years," he gasped as they left the main lobby.

Unable to explain further, he dropped his arm and bent forward, laughing with what could only be classified as a tremendous belly laugh. Trying to explain, and bring his laughter under control, he said, "When I was seventeen years old, and the male equivalent of a virgin, I took a sweet young thing to a motel." He gasped in deep breaths of air. "When the desk clerk asked if we were honeymooners . . ." Laughter wouldn't allow him to finish.

"What happened?" Elizabeth asked, starting to smile.

"We fled. The desk clerk was an old poker buddy of my dad's." His short speech was punctuated with more belly laughs.

She could imagine the scene with a young Jared running out of the motel, dragging a teenage girl behind, with the motel clerk shouting, "Ante up." Laughter swept through them like a highly contagious disease.

"Stop, Jared! You're making my sides hurt."

They had both braced themselves against the interior glass wall as they tried to regain their composure.

"Let's get out of here before someone else comes along." Lacing his fingers between hers, Jared pulled Elizabeth behind his long strides.

"Slow down, or we'll really cause a scene when I fall flat on my face at your feet," she laughingly complained.

Shortening his strides, but still laughing, he escorted her out of the air-conditioned comfort into the humid, sultry, Houston night air.

An elderly car attendant crossed in front of them, smiling at the attractive couple. "I didn't know they had a comedian up there," he commented.

Jared slapped his thigh and began laughing again. "A comedian," he choked. "The silver Mercedes, please," he told the attendant.

"Yes, sir!" the grinning attendant replied, giving a mock salute.

Pushing her knuckles into her mouth, Eliza-

71

beth tried to stop the giggles. She was laughing with Jared, but also at herself. When he asked for the car she realized phoning Sara would have been futile. She had driven her car to pick Jared up, and Sara's car was in the repair shop. The fates would have blocked any attempt to escape.

"Come on, Jared," she said as the car pulled up. "Let's get out of here before we're arrested for public intoxication."

The car door was opened for her by the attendant as Jared stumbled around to the driver's side. Moments later he flopped into the car, breathing deeply.

Watching him loosen his tie, strip it off, and hang it on the rearview mirror, Elizabeth realized his tale of sexual naiveté was not only amusing, it was endearing. The cynical, self-assured, virile image had been dropped, replaced by a lovable, laughing man, willing to share what must have been a humiliating experience.

"I haven't laughed this hard in years," he commented with a boyish smile. "You're good for me."

Fluidly he dropped the car into gear, turned off the tape deck, then covered her hand on the leather seat with his.

"Come on D.D.H., move over," he demanded softly.

"D.D.H?"

"Damned Door Hugger. That's what we used to call girls who wouldn't sit close."

"Far be it from me to be a D.D.H.," Elizabeth quipped, sliding to the center of the seat.

"Hmm. Nice. Not safe, but nice," he said, draping his arm over her shoulder, drawing her closer.

"Nice enough to make you a beggar?" she teased, anticipating his touch. When his arm tensed, then withdrew, she knew without looking that the smile had vanished.

"How stupid of me not to realize your eagerness was a trap," he scathingly retorted, shifting away from bodily contact.

"I was joking!" Elizabeth exclaimed, inching closer. "Can't you take a joke?"

Harsh laughter froze her desire to eliminate the space between them. "Okay, lady, I believe you." The tone of his voice belied his words. "To prove you were kidding, let's hear *you* beg."

The stranger beside her was the despicable man in the restaurant booth, the owner of Gems Unlimited, who had manipulated her into making the bet in the first place. He certainly wasn't the sensuous man on the dance floor, or the warm, laughing man outside the hotel. This cold, withdrawn stranger was insulting her again!

"Cat got your tongue?" he jibed at her delayed response. "Come on, honey. Don't disappoint me now. You're confirming my suspicions. You did intend having a quick victory, didn't you?"

Sliding back to the passenger's side, Elizabeth evaded the snarling question. She had vowed,

73

repeatedly, to drive him to his knees. How could she deny it? Lying would compound the felony.

"Didn't you?" Jared questioned, demanding a response.

"Yes!" The curt monosyllable was delivered with a cool aloofness that hid the pain he had inflicted. *He wants to think the worst of me, darn it. Let him.*

"You planned on enticing the 'rutting bull' to the slaughterhouse, then pitch him out on his ear, didn't you?"

"Yes." *But that was before* . . . The need to defend herself was wiped away by his scornful laugh.

"You are a witch, Elizabeth Sheffield. A cold-hearted, hard, conniving witch."

Elizabeth inwardly flinched at each bitterly delivered word. Hadn't he called her a witch when he held her on the dance floor? What a different meaning the same word had now. *Well,* she decided, *if he wants a witch, I'll give him one.*

"The witch's nest is in the Edgeview condos. Since we're in *my* broomstick, fly it in a southerly direction, please."

"Someday I'll cut out that sharp tongue and serve it to you for breakfast . . . in bed," he promised.

"Eat in bed, sleep with crumbs," she glibly retorted, anger replacing hurt.

The overhead streetlights cast an ominous glow on his grim features. Strong hands alternated clenching, then relaxing, on the steering wheel.

With a twist of her wrist she opened the glove compartment and selected a cassette. Seconds later, loud rock and roll music boomed into the car's otherwise silent interior. If nothing else, pride demanded she have the last cutting word, even if the blade had a double edge.

CHAPTER FOUR

"Lizzy. Get up. Your dad's here."

Groggily Elizabeth heard someone urging her to get out of bed, but couldn't coordinate the words with any meaning. Feeling her shoulder being vigorously shaken, she rolled away from the rocking motion.

"Elizabeth! You're father is in the kitchen waiting for you. Come . . . on . . . he's leaving town."

Rolling onto her back, she tried to open her eyes, but couldn't. The lashes were stuck together. "Get me a washcloth, please. I seem to have been struck blind by the cosmetic industry."

She felt the weight removed from the edge of her bed, followed shortly by the sound of splashing water. Footsteps, which should have been a padded muffled sound, crashed through her head.

"You look awful," Sara said as she inspected the smear under each of Elizabeth's eyelids.

"Whisper. No loud noises, please." The pounding increased when she levered herself into a semi-upright position. Champagne, she groaned silently, never again. The demons with bass drums were trying to split her skull in half. The cool, damp washcloth was more welcome than rain in the desert.

"Where's the army?" she inquired hoarsely.

"What army?"

"The one that camped in my mouth last night?" Elizabeth moaned in an attempt to kill the drummers with a smile.

Sara approached with a glass of water and two aspirin. For once Elizabeth was thankful Sara was next door and had a key. Grimacing as she swallowed the pills, she realized Sara was anxious to hear about her victory in the Battle of the Double Standard.

"George has a flight to catch. Hop up and I'll turn the shower on for you."

"Hop?" Elizabeth asked incredulously. "Crawl. That is my only possible mode of locomotion, and that's iffy."

"Lean on me." Removing the cloth from her limp hand, Sara shoved one arm between the pillow and Elizabeth's shoulders.

"I told your dad when I heard him banging on your door, you were recovering from a heavy date last night. I can hardly wait to hear about it," she bubbled as she nudged Elizabeth's groaning body into the lukewarm shower.

Water pelted her face, shoulders, and uptilted breasts. Revolving slowly, the steady stream ran over her hair, buttocks, and legs, washing away a portion of her discomfort.

Don't think, her brain pleaded. *A simple child's puzzle will blow all circuits.*

Minutes later, hair in a towel turban, face clean and shiny, garbed in a serviceable quilted robe, she presented herself in the kitchen.

"You appear to be recovering from your bout of bottle virus," George said in a teasing voice as he swiftly assessed the damage. "Sit down. You have a choice of 'the hair of the dog' or strong black coffee."

"Coffee. I couldn't stand to look at an empty tomato juice glass. Only an empty buttermilk glass would be worse," she answered, reaching for the coffee and rejecting the Bloody Mary.

George glanced at his watch, tapping the crystal. Although he inventoried thousands of watches, he wore the unreliable timepiece his wife had given him on their twentieth anniversary.

"I dropped by to tell you I'm leaving for Brazil, and to give you a credit slip."

"Tweedledum and Tweedledee bought the opals, I presume?" she asked, gulping down the first swallow of steamy liquid..

"Right." Leaning forward, he inspected her face more closely. "Are you certain you aren't coming down with something?"

78

Should she tell her dad the love bug had nibbled on her neck last night? "No, Dad. I'll survive, even though it looks as though death is imminent."

George kissed her cheek.

"I've left a number by the telephone, Sara," he said, a wide smile splitting his face. "If the patient croaks, notify me and I'll wire flowers."

"Thanks a lot, Dad," she replied sarcastically, then chuckled.

George started to say something, changed his mind, picked up his briefcase, and as he left tossed out, "See you."

Holding her cup of coffee, Sara sat down next to her friend. Unable to contain her curiosity a moment longer, she demanded with a mischievous twinkle, "Spill."

"Disasterville. He knew who I was the whole time and manipulated me into a wager I'm not certain I can win."

"Yes?" Sara probed, her curiosity further piqued.

"I bet him I could get him into my bed before he could get me into his. If I win, he produces my designs my way; if he wins, my designs go into mass production."

"Wow! Anybody win yet?"

"Not yet. We ended the evening hurling insults at each other and retired to our respective beds . . . alone."

"Oh, goodie," Sara enthused, rubbing her

palms together, then slapping her thighs. "We are really going to have some fun with this one."

"Was that a royal 'we' or do you have a frog in your pocket?" Elizabeth teased, pouring herself a warm-up.

"We, as in us. It was my brainstorm to answer the ad. You can't shut me out now!"

"Aptly put. That is exactly my intention." Pointing to the door, she said, "Don't let the doorknob hit you in the rump as you leave."

"But, Elizabeth, you can't do that to me!" Sara wailed, heartstricken. "You'll need me to help plot his downfall. Besides, you promised to go with me to Galveston today!"

"Okay. I'll keep my promise, but you have to concentrate on your own lovelife and stay out of mine," she warned, tucking a damp strand of hair back under the turban.

"Given a choice, I'd rather stay here and plot," Sara cheekily responded as she jauntily popped off the kitchen chair and headed toward the front door.

The doorbell pealed as Sara put her hand on the knob. Before the last ding had rung, she swung the door open. Her eyes and mouth rounded in surprise when she saw a tall, handsome stranger pull his finger away from the doorbell. Dressed casually in jeans and a cool cotton shirt, he stood there with a single long-stemmed red rose in one hand. Spying Elizabeth seated at the breakfast table, he brushed past Sara, strode the width of the room, dropped to one knee in front of Elizabeth, bowed his head, and stuck the flower forward.

"Forgive me?"

Elizabeth was speechless. Was he begging on bended knee? The crinkles around his eyes and the tiny lift of the corners of his mouth told her the apology was sincere, but he wasn't begging.

"Well?" his husky baritone voice asked.

Recovering her voice, Elizabeth plucked the rose from his hand, then batted the bloom against his cheek softly. "Forgiven, cad. Get off your knee. Jared McKnight," she gestured toward Sara, "I'd like for you to meet Sara, the lady who answered your mistress ad with my résumé."

His head swiveled in the direction of the door as he lithely rose to his feet. "Perhaps you should have answered the ad yourself," he said suavely, extending his hand in her direction.

"Silver-tongued devil, isn't he?" Sara asked Elizabeth as she placed her hand into his outstretched palm. Before releasing it, Sara turned it over and glanced at the lines on the palm. "I see a tall strawberry-blonde entering your life," she murmured mysteriously. "And a short, eventful trip . . . miles and miles of water."

"Sara," Elizabeth said in a warning tone, "you're doing it again." Seeing the blatant look of innocence on her friend's face, she explained to Jared, "We planned on going to Galveston today. In Sara's not-so-subtle way, she's inviting you along."

"Do you mind?" he asked, taking advantage of the opportunity to be with her.

Shrugging her shoulders and glancing toward Sara, she avoided answering the direct question by saying, "Pushy devil, aren't you?"

"It's not every day I have the chance to squire two such lovely damsels," he answered urbanely, including a round-eyed Sara in the compliment.

"Suave too," Sara injected. "Have a seat and we'll take your proposal under advisement."

Elizabeth knew Sara enjoyed puns, but did she have to stress the word *proposal*. She could see the wheels spinning in her friend's head. She was hatching a new plot already!

"Sara, shouldn't you be running along to get your suit on?" she suggested, wanting to get her out of the apartment before she could add to the palm-reading she had started earlier.

"Oh, yes. My swimsuit," Sara stammered, shifting from one stout leg to the other. "I really hate to break my promise, but I won't be able to go." Leaning out the open doorway, she added, "I have to run. I hear my mother calling."

"From Dallas?" Elizabeth blurted out in disbelief.

Sara shot her friend a disparaging look. "My mother is calling" was their standard excuse for departing when an interesting male appeared on the scene.

"You know she calls long-distance on Saturday," she replied, covering up Elizabeth's gaffe. "Have a good time and don't step on any sand castles," she called, backing out the door and hastily closing it.

Elizabeth heard an amused chuckle coming from Jared. Why was he laughing? Did he see through her friend's ruse? Not completely cured of her hangover, she asked testily, "Somebody rattle your cage?"

"Sara did," he answered, not allowing her tartness to sour their newfound peace. "I wouldn't be a bit surprised to learn she's an orphan. She's a poor liar."

Elizabeth grinned, relieved to know she wasn't the brunt of his laughter. "What she lacks in acting ability she compensates for in inventiveness." Once again conscious of her state of deshabille, she patted the damp turban on her head, and said, "If you'll excuse me, I'll get ready."

Green eyes swept from the coil of terry cloth on her head to the bare toes sticking out from under the hem of her robe. Adequately, if improperly, clothed, she felt as though he had x-ray vision and was enjoying the view. Remembering the assessing glance he had raked over her in his office, she noted the stone harshness was missing.

Today is going to be better, she thought. *I can feel it in my bones.*

CHAPTER FIVE

The white heat from the blazing summer sun bore down ferociously as they left the building. Being a native Houstonian, Elizabeth wished the Gulf breeze extended across the fifty miles separating the city from the coast.

"Let's take my car," Elizabeth suggested. "I have beach blankets and a cooler already in the trunk."

"Fine. I'm an inveterate beach bum. I always keep a swimsuit and towel in my car. I'll go get them." He disappeared around the corner, and in a few moments returned carrying the swimsuit and towel.

On their drive neither Elizabeth nor Jared brought up the disaster of the previous day. A temporary truce was in effect. Each was content to find out inconsequential information about the other.

Approaching Galveston Island, they exchanged trivia about it. The 1900 hurricane that wiped out the Wall Street of the Southwest was of primary interest to both of them. Jared scoffed at the ignorance of the people who had gone to the beach to watch the hurricane come in. Their foolishness had cost them their lives.

As the car approached Seawall Boulevard, Jared asked, "Which way? Left to Stewart Beach and the South Jetty, or right to San Luis Pass?"

"Right. Sand Pocket Park would be lovely."

Aside from the showers available, they would also have more privacy. She realized he was asking for more than directions. He was giving her the choice of being surrounded by a crowd of fun-seeking, Frisbee-throwing teenagers who frequented both Stewart Beach and the south end of the island, or the more deserted beaches at the other end. Flashing her a brilliant smile, he turned right at the stop light.

Long fishing piers stretched into the Gulf of Mexico on their left. Men, women, and children stood patiently watching their lines. Each was certain the next tug on the heavy monofilament would be "the big one." Jared commented that he had drowned many a shrimp while standing on that pier, but the big one inevitably rejected his bait in favor of the person's next to him.

Elizabeth felt more than the original physical pull on her heartstrings. The stories he had woven were warm and caring. His keen sense of humor made the dry facts into living, breathing events.

I like him, she mused, studying his strong features from behind dark sunglasses. The combination of liking and the magnetic physical appeal amounted to what? She knew the answer, but guilt pinched and clawed from within. By playing the role of seductress the previous evening, she had gone past the point of their relationship being built on a misunderstanding. She had intentionally tried to hurt him. "Destroy the male ego" had been her battle cry. Make him feel lower than a flea on a lizard's belly.

How wrong I was, she thought. Granted, he'd concealed the fact that he knew who she was and had managed to catch her in her own trap, but there had been no malice involved on his part.

She'd use their time together today to right the wrongs, and convince him to use her designs in limited-edition copies. It would be possible if she could convince him working with gold was a craft. Mentally she recited the arguments she'd use when presenting her designs to other companies. Wasn't a pen drawing of more value than a lithograph? A designer dress better constructed than one bought off the rack? A Persian rug made by skilled craftsmen was treasured long after a machine-made carpet was discarded.

The designs Jared had were conceived by an artist. Would he expect Picasso to stand in line and paint a small portion of a picture? Didn't he realize when she designed a piece of jewelry she used stones and metal to produce a canvas people could touch? Her designs were unusual because she looked for stones with uniqueness and color. They were pieces of color and textures brought together much as a stained-glass artist uses pieces of color to produce an effect for a cathedral.

I'm an artist, she silently stated, *not a production jeweler. I fall in love with every piece I make. Wasn't this the same feeling Elsa Peretti and Paloma Picasso had?* Someday, if she avoided the lure of quick profits and mass-produced designs, her work would be as well known as that of her idols.

The daydream ended as Jared stopped the car to pay the two-dollar parking fee at the entrance of Sand Pocket Beach. Parking the car in a vacant space near the cedar building that housed the concession stand, Jared said with a wry smile, "Back on earth again I see."

"One of the disadvantages of living in Space City," she quipped, thankful he hadn't offered to pay a penny for her thoughts.

Reaching over her legs, he twisted the knob that opened the glove compartment and popped the trunk . . . all without touching her.

With a twisted smile he said in answer to her questioning look, "I promised myself I'd be a good boy and keep my Roman hands and Russian fingers off you."

Gaily Elizabeth laughed. She hadn't heard that expression in years. "Am I not to have any say in the no-touch policy?" she inquired with impish delight.

"Not this time. You wouldn't want a man without honor or self-control, would you?" he bantered.

Seriousness was lying beneath the surface. Flesh covered the man, but underneath there was a steel inner core. He was testing his own strength.

"No," she murmured. "Last night you made me . . . aware of the danger of moving too fast." Levelly gazing into his eyes, she decided to meet him halfway with a full measure of honesty.

"I'm a dangerous man?" Laugh lines around his eyes deepened. "How intriguing. Your compliments are delicious." His eyes lowered to her lips.

Elizabeth was kissed without being touched. A tender, caring kiss that hinted of the passionate fires being kept under tight control. Her own fingertips lightly brushed over her lower lip. Small front teeth bit the inside of the bowed lip. *He is dangerous*, she mused. *Few men could make love effectively with their eyes.*

"Let's go," he said with a deep chuckle. "While we still can."

Gathering their paraphernalia, they dashed up the steps and down the scorching wooden planks to the sandy beach. The wind tossed her hair, catching the golden highlights. Removing her sandals, she scrunched the sand particles between pink-tipped toes.

"Mmm. I must have been a sea creature in some previous life." Arms flung wide as if to embrace the white-capped water, she said, "I love the sand and the surf."

"A lovely creature with golden skin reflecting the sun," he replied softly, the sound of his voice nearly covered by the pounding of the surf against the beach.

Disrobing quickly, Elizabeth dashed into the surf, not slowing her pace until she was waist-deep. Diving through an oncoming wave, resurfacing, then diving again, Elizabeth frolicked in the warm, salty water. The initial spurt of exuberance waning, she rolled to her back, allowing the buoyancy of the water to support her.

"Don't go away," Jared shouted, waving his trunks and sprinting back to the bathhouse with the ease and coordination of a well-trained athlete.

Relaxing, Elizabeth allowed the waves to carry her toward the beach. Eyes closed, she enjoyed nature's fingers gently pushing her in one direction, then tugging her the other way as the wave receded. When something grazed against her arm, she jackknifed away.

"Jared," she squealed in protest when she realized he had dragged a piece of seaweed over her arm. "I thought you were a man-of-war." Forcefully she splashed sea water on his face to wash away the grin.

"Want to play rough, huh?"

Using both hands, he slapped the surface repeatedly. Water splashed into her face. Having taken a breath at the wrong time, she choked as the salty water went up her nose.

"I give," she sputtered between coughs. "I give!"

Immediately his hands stilled. "Sorry, I can't wipe the salt water away from your eyes, but you know the rules." Long fingers waggled in front of her face.

Then he flopped back and swam away from her as she struggled to get the long rope of hair and the salt water out of her eyes. Wading toward the shore, feeling the sand being tugged from beneath her feet by the undertow, she watched Jared cut through the waves. The water clinging to the tips of her eyelashes acted as prisms that surrounded his graceful strokes in brilliant shades of yellow, green, and blue. She took a deep breath and the tangy salt air filled her nostrils, completing the picture.

"You're beautiful, Jared McKnight," she said softly out loud. Kicking at the froth on the shallow water at the beachline, she regretted his self-imposed restriction. She wanted to touch what she had dreamed about on the dance floor. Seeing the dark-golden tones of flesh beneath the dark hair on his chest had her fingers itching again.

The heat of the sand beneath her bare feet began burning her soles. Racing to their pile of towels, she raised her arms high and allowed the wind to billow a brilliantly red beach blanket on the sand. Sprawling on her stomach, the warm wind and the hot sun dried her skin and fluffed the tips of her hair.

"Redheads in teeny polka-dot bikinis burn easily, don't they?" The unfamiliar voice came from a tall blond giant standing at the bottom edge of the blanket.

Go away, she thought. Eyes blinking the salt off her lashes, she replied icily, "Not Texas redheads. And it's not red." She hated labels such as Redhead and Carrot Top.

Turning toward the water, she saw Jared lithely running toward them. *What will he think if this hunk of masculinity won't go away before he gets here? Guess I'm about to find out.* She groaned inwardly when the giant moved closer to the towel and Jared rapidly closed the gap.

Halting less than a foot from the intruder, Jared planted his hands on his narrow hips and spread his legs apart to balance his weight.

"Private property," he stated, barely moving his lips.

The younger, more muscle-bound stranger assessed his opponent, glanced at Elizabeth, made a slight snort, then sprinted down the beach. Elizabeth felt her skin burn as Jared's eyes went from sand-covered toes slowly over the skimpy yellow swimsuit to her windblown hair. She'd worn similar suits every year, but his smoldering gaze made her aware that only the essential areas were covered. Cheeks flushing, she felt deliciously, wickedly, enticingly . . . nude.

"If I can't touch, I'll be damned if any other man is going to have the privilege."

The menacing tone in his voice left no doubt as to his meaning. Dropping to his knees, he leaned back on his haunches, and, fanning his fingers through dark wet hair, shook out the salt water. Droplets fell, splattering her.

"Keep it up, you shaggy dog, and I'll lock you in the car," she threatened while laughing.

Lying down on his side, he propped his head up, feasting on the shadowed valley between her breasts. A broad grin split his face as he fell back and closed his eyes.

Smiling with satisfaction, Elizabeth let her eyes travel over territory previously hidden by business suits. He was one of those few men who looked better without his clothing than with. Not one ounce of superfluous flesh covered his frame. There was enough dark hair matting his chest to be masculine, without reminding her of a hairy beast.

"You're smiling in that funny way again. One day soon you're going to tell me what is humorous about my body."

"Anybody as ugly as you are should be used to peculiar smiles," she teased.

"Ugly! That's three insults in one day. You accept my rose with 'cad,' call me a pushy devil, and now I'm reduced to being ugly. My ego is irreparably damaged."

"Poor darling. Unmercifully persecuted by the opposite sex, aren't you?" Pseudo-pity coated her sarcastic reply.

"Only by you, sweet creature from the sea." The teasing evaporated. Once again his eyes shut.

"Are you tired, or bored? I must be losing my touch," she complained softly.

"Elizabeth! I'm *struggling* to keep from touching you. Be a good girl and shut up. Better yet, cover up."

Seeing the whiteness around his clamped lips, she rolled to her stomach and muttered, "It's tough on me too!"

"Put some sunscreen on your back if you aren't going to cover up," he instructed, ignoring her gripe.

"Not being a contortionist or double-jointed makes that impossible," she replied curtly.

"Damned if I do, and damned if I don't," he muttered, rolling his eyes heavenward.

"Do it. I won't appreciate being returned to Houston resembling a boiled crab!"

The odor of coconut oil filled her senses as the creamy lotion was squirted over her shoulders. Smooth hands swiped the protective liquid over her back and shoulders. The whole process took less than ten seconds.

Disappointment made Elizabeth wince as Jared

lay back down. She had anticipated sensuous fingertips lingering as they smoothed the lotion into her hot flesh. She felt cheated and irritable.

"Thanks," she huffed.

"It was nothing."

That's for sure, she mentally agreed. Peeking through her lashes, she saw a smug smirk on Jared's lips. *Tease! We'll see who has the last laugh.* Deliberately she twisted onto her back, shifting first her shoulders, then her buttocks.

"Quit squirming," he barked.

Elizabeth smirked.

The two supple bodies remained close, but not touching. Sea gulls swooped from the sky in search of bits of food. When lucky in their quest they soared up from the water, beaks clasping a shrimp or small fish. Couples strolled, some touching, others not.

Jared linked his little finger with hers. The circuit was complete, causing small electrical tingles to shoot up her arm. What was it about this man that made the slightest touch a meaningful caress? Feminine intuition told her his restraint was his way of making up for his callous words. He wanted her to know she was more than a receptacle for physical lust. An inner glow swept through her at this realization. *Maybe, just maybe*, she fervently prayed, *we can work it out.*

"Elizabeth?" Jared's husky drawl brought her away from her fantasies. "We need to talk."

Stretching, she propped her head up on one

arm. "I'm listening," she said while covering a yawn with one hand.

"I want you to design for Gems Unlimited. I also want you to make arrangements for and hostess a reception next weekend. Can you do it?"

Not commenting, Elizabeth brushed dried sand from her forearms. Was this the time to clarify her position as an artist, or would it be exterminating an anthill with a hydrogen bomb? Would the fallout result in neither of them getting what they wanted? Somehow she knew this was the wrong time to push for limited editions of her designs.

"Your silence is not making this easy." Lines crinkled upward as he smiled with his eyes. "At least grunt so I know you hear me."

"Uhnt."

"This week you'll spend most of your time working on the reception. I'm certain you've handled similar functions for your father. Can you handle it for me?"

"Uhnt."

"Not funny, Elizabeth." He chuckled at his closely followed directions.

"Three times for yes, two for no."

"Uhnt! Uhnt!"

A frown marred his brow. A teasing smile was plastered on Elizabeth's face.

"UHNT!"

Deep laughter rang out joyfully. Victory

stamped his features and his eyes glittered like freshly minted dimes.

"You have my word of honor. I won't do anything you don't want me to." He bent forward to seal the bargain as they had at their first meeting, then pulled back. With one finger he crossed his heart instead.

Scanning her wardrobe, Elizabeth puzzled over the appropriate suit to wear. Instead of reporting directly to Jared, she was to see Mary McKnight, the personnel director.

CHAPTER SIX

Scanning her wardrobe, Elizabeth puzzled over the appropriate suit to wear. Instead of reporting directly to Jared, she was to see Mary McKnight, the personnel director. Why was it necessary to go through the personnel department when Jared had already hired her?

"Jared and Mary McKnight," she muttered.

Was Mary McKnight the sister who put the ad in the paper? Couldn't be. McKnight wouldn't be her surname. What, if any, relationship existed between Jared and Mary?

"That's all I need to do. Fall for a married man." Was he seeking an illicit relationship with stamp of approval from his wife? The advertisement *had* been for a mistress.

If only she had read the name he had written on the back of his business card Saturday, instead of earlier this morning, the mystery would have been solved. A simple, direct question would have saved the gnashing of teeth that threatened to loosen and grind them to the gum line.

Saturday, after coming back from Galveston, thoughts of extracting a future date had preoccupied her mind. When Jared told her he would be with his parents Sunday, and wouldn't be able to see her, disappointment and frustration surpassed any feelings of curiosity. He had departed without even a good-night kiss.

The hands-off policy had tested Jared's honor and her own frustration level. His restraint had driven her straight up the proverbial wall. She respected self-control, but respect hadn't eliminated the desire to be held and kissed.

Sara's oohs and aahs hadn't helped ease the frustration either. She thought the no-touching policy would make winning the bet easier. Jared should be forbidden fruit. The only satisfaction Elizabeth had was crunching, slurping, and smacking her way through two golden delicious apples Sunday night. Symbolically she destroyed Sara's strategy.

Elizabeth solved her immediate problem by selecting a navy blue suit, tailored white blouse, and matching navy shoes from the closet. John Molloy would have been proud of her choice. She was dressing for success. The outfit would be conservative enough for a wife, sister, or mother.

With trepidation Elizabeth entered the outer

office of the personnel department. Card in hand, she approached the receptionist.

"May I help you?"

"Yes." Extending the business card forward, she said "I have an appointment with Ms. McKnight."

Ms. was nondescript. It consciously removed the title of married woman, and provided a temporary solution to the puzzle. She hoped the receptionist would correct the Ms. with Miss.

"She's anxiously awaiting your arrival," the smiling brunette responded. "Would you go down the short hall to your left? Her office is the last door. Good luck."

"She" and "her" didn't provide the missing clue. Elizabeth wanted to quiz the friendly woman, but was not given the opportunity. The receptionist pushed the intercom button, nodded her head in the direction of the hallway, and informed her employer that Elizabeth Sheffield was on her way.

"Ms. McKnight?" Elizabeth inquired, entering the office.

"You're Elizabeth. You may not know it, but you're going to save my marriage." A bespeckled, brown-haired woman extended her hand in greeting.

Cripes. He is married.

"Jared certainly knows how to pick them," Mary continued. The uptilted lips hid amusement.

Grasping the small hand firmly, Elizabeth replied, "Thank you. You, too, are an attractive choice."

Bewilderment flashed over the face behind the desk. "But, my dear, Jared wasn't given any choice about me."

An arranged marriage? Is that why she agreed to her husband hiring a mistress? Nauseated, dropping the hand, Elizabeth sank into the office chair in front of the desk. Her worst fears were about to be confirmed. As badly as she needed a larger market for her designs, she would have to find an excuse to justify quitting before starting.

"I'm Jared's sister," the woman explained. "I still use my maiden name for expediency here at work. It's my marriage *to Steve* I'm trying to patch up."

Elizabeth's spirits began to soar. Swallowing, the nauseous knot disappeared. The blood that had drained from her face began circulating, following its normal course.

"Thank goodness the stricken look has left your face," Mary said as she chuckled. "I thought for a moment I was going to have to call the company nurse!"

"I'm a lousy poker player," Elizabeth said, relaxing enough to cross her legs at the knee.

"Just to set the record straight, I put that ad in the paper. Jared nearly blew a gasket when I told him I'd advertised for a mistress. Quite frankly he has thwarted all my matchmaking efforts, and my perverted sense of humor made me cross out social secretary and write in mistress." Removing her glasses as she spoke, Elizabeth could see a mischievous twinkle in the green eyes that matched her sibling's. The quirk in Mary's mouth resembled his also.

"Forgive me for causing the original mix-up?" she coaxed. "I'm tight-mouthed about my personal problems here at work, but I decided to reveal part of the problem to you right off the bat."

"Forgiven." After removing two of her greatest fears, she would have forgiven Mary anything. Woman's intuition hadn't failed her after all. Jared wasn't the type of person to advertise for a mistress. He wasn't married. All the wringing of hands and the mental gymnastics of a not-too-bright ten-year-old had been for nothing.

"Now to business."

Mary replaced the dark-rimmed glasses on her straight nose, pushing them to the bridge with a quick poke of her forefinger. She slid several typewritten pages over the desk toward Elizabeth.

"That's Jared's agenda. Take a quick glance. Ask any questions you think I'll be able to help you with."

One item dominated the list. RECEPTION: TWENTY-FIVE COUPLES. SATURDAY. The words were printed in red capital letters. A tall order on short notice, Elizabeth thought. The second page contained a list of caterers, florists, rental companies, and other sundry names. The third page was a diagram, resembling a miniature hand-drawn blueprint.

"Whose house is this?" Elizabeth asked.

"My parents' dream house. Dad ran the company until two years ago. He had a minor heart attack. Jared took over and my folks retired to west Texas."

The explanation was tersely given. Elizabeth wanted more personal information, but decided to wait until it was volunteered.

The last typewritten pages held names, addresses, and phone numbers.

"Friends or business associates?" she queried when she saw Tweedledee's and Tweedledum's names.

"A mixture of both. Dad is formally handing the reins over to Jared." The mischievous twinkle returned. "One of many reasons for the reception. It is also an excuse for me to invite my estranged spouse to a social gathering."

Elizabeth noticed Mary was doodling intertwining circles on a scratch pad. Meticulously she placed a dot in every other circle.

Completing the last row, she self-consciously put the pencil down. "I know Jared badgered you into helping him out with this project. Will there be any problems?"

"I hope not, but you both realize I'm not a social secretary. I'm a jewelry designer."

Mary sighed. "Jared mentioned using one of your designs on a new project he has started, but frankly your work hours this week will be spent making arrangements for the reception." Pulling the doodle forward, closer to her chest, she asked, "You can spare a week away from the drafting table, can't you?"

What's a week in a lifetime? she thought when she saw the parallel lines of strain over Mary's glasses. *The woman is distraught.* Jared had referred to a businessman adapting to and playing many roles; Mary hadn't been able to adapt as easily. Momentarily she wondered if there were other pressures on Mary she wasn't revealing.

"Can I call on you if I run into any snags?" Elizabeth asked, not certain she could set up a reception of this size in a week.

"By all means. If you need anything, including a shoulder to cry on when Brother Jared is being impossible, give me a buzz." A dimple on one side of Mary's cheek appeared as her lips spread into a wide smile and the lines on her brow were erased. "The plant is located off Telephone Road, but your temporary office is upstairs next to big brother's." The dimple grew larger. "In fact, there is a connecting door between the two offices."

The desk chair squeaked as Elizabeth swiveled round and round. She felt like a small child when allowed to enter a grownup's office. Mary was expecting a minor miracle, but she had also stocked the desk with all the necessary tools to complete the task. It contained pens, pencils, purchase orders, and any other small item neces-

103

sary to insure efficiency. A large leatherbound calendar dominated the desktop. The words GEMS UNLIMITED, elegantly centered in golden letters of the outside cover, gave Elizabeth kinesthetic pleasure as her fingers traced over them.

Realizing how foolish she would appear if Jared dropped in, she began outlining whom she needed to contact with fierce determination. She would be straining her organizational abilities to the hilt. After this week the pace would slow down and she envisioned herself spending most of the day in the workshop and maybe an hour or so updating Jared's schedule. Running between the office and the workshop, back and forth, she would resemble a dog chasing its tail.

She spent the entire morning on the telephone contacting the caterer, florist, and the shop that had been recommended to print the invitations. As Elizabeth had suspected, they had all been used on previous occasions. This made her job easier. They were familiar with the particular needs and tastes of the McKnight family.

Between calls Elizabeth glanced at the communicating door. *Where is Jared?* She could hear him. She knew he was in the adjoining office working. Why hadn't he welcomed his new employee? A frown marred her smooth forehead. Had he lost interest so soon?

At eleven o'clock her stomach growled ominously. *Sounds as though the big ones are eating the little ones,* she mused, rubbing the noisy area. *Maybe the hermit next door will feed me.* Purposefully she strode to and opened the communicating door.

"Jared?"

Swiveling, he turned toward her.

"Yes, Elizabeth," he answered, a welcoming smile accompanying his words. "I wondered how long it would take you to open that door. How's it going?"

Her heart thumping in response to his smile, she answered, "Super. How about letting me buy the boss lunch?"

The smile ceased to exist. "Not today." Briskness bordered on being abrasive.

She had not expected a negative reply. Her perky smile was erased by his succinct refusal but pride kept her shoulders straight.

"Can you cook?" Jared asked as he crossed to stand in front of her.

"With a can opener and a stove, I can warm up anything."

"That the best you can do?"

His left arm was strategically placed against the edge of the bookcase by the door. Elizabeth was between Jared and the wall, completely trapped as his other arm extended and leaned against the doorjamb.

Elizabeth lifted her chin. The old line, Kiss me, you fool, crossed her mind. "Yes," crossed her lips, answering his question.

Jared studied her, seemingly fascinated by the curve of her lower lip. His head lowered an infinitesimal fraction. Smoky green eyes reflected

Elizabeth's enticing, darkening, brown eyes. Jared moved lower, obviously wanting to caress her parting lips. The cloth of her blouse caressed the silken sheen of his shirt fleetingly. Elizabeth anticipated closer contact. Her breathing was no longer even, as short, silent breaths fed her lungs.

Lightly she placed her hands on his waist, pulling him forward. She felt his thighs tense as they touched her skirt. Warm breath feathered her hair, causing her scalp to tingle. Sensitive to his closeness, she longed to pull him closer. Her stomach growled loudly.

"You'd better go feed yourself," he said abruptly in a controlled voice as he pushed away from the wall.

"But Jared—"

"I have work to do," he interrupted briskly.

She felt as though she had plunged five-hundred feet downward in an elevator with a snapped cable. Gasping audibly, she turned toward her own office.

"Elizabeth?"

Her skirt twirled attractively around slender legs as she eagerly turned.

"Would you fix dinner for us tonight? My place? I'd cook, but I'm lousy at it." His voice was strained and hoarse rather than brisk.

"Yes. When and where?"

"Seven?" Ripping a sheet of paper from a pad, he scribbled his address on it and handed the sheet to her. He did not allow their fingers to touch. "The doorman will let you in."

Folding the paper, she tucked it into the front of her blouse. Satisfaction swept through her as his hands clenched. He was still adhering to the touch-me-not philosophy.

"See you later," she quipped, and swiftly left.

The apple in her purse would appease her cravings, wouldn't it?

A bawdy college tune rambled around in her head as she put the finishing touches on a pork chop casserole. The afternoon had sped by. Her usual blue Monday dinner with Sara was canceled by a quick, uninformative call to the bank. Why did that song keep tantalizing her memory? When she recalled the words, she silently laughed to herself.

Singing with gusto, her contralto voice echoed off the silent pale walls. Curious about the unexplored parts of the town house, she climbed the carpeted steps, singing as she went:

> I wish I was a fascinating witch,
> I'd never be poor and I'd always be rich.

Pushing the partially closed door open wider at the top of the steps, she entered a masculine bedroom decorated in navy blues and beiges. The massive, king-size fruitwood furniture, highly polished, was pleasing to the eye. The room was neat and orderly.

> I'd live in a house so clean and white,
> But on the corner there would be a red light.

Her tune was interrupted by giggles as she re-called Jared mistakenly thinking she was a lady of ill repute.

> Every year I'd take a vacation,
> And leave my clientele to da-dee-da-da.
> But once a year, I'd go hog wild . . .

She entered an all-white, spotless tiled bath-room.

> And have myself an illegitimate child.

Returning to the master suite, she plumped the huge pillows.

> I wish I was a fascinating witch . . .
> Instead of a gosh-darned virgin.

The reality of the lyrics corresponding with her desires caused her to sprawl across the width of the inviting bed.

"Is that an invitation?"

Jared stood at the door, leaning against the frame, one ankle casually crossed over the other. Loosening his tie and unbuttoning his shirt to the waist, he advanced into the dimly lit room.

"Jared," she choked out when her tongue fell

from the top of her mouth. "You're early," she squeaked. "I'm not ready." Scrambling to get off the bed, she could see that he was.

Long arms and the length of his body blocked her escape route. "Are you a virgin, little golden sea creature?" he crooned into her ear softly.

Relaxing under his muscular frame, she answered, "Do I look as though I grew up in a nunnery?" A wink answered the question.

Gathering her close, his lips touched hers with a sigh. The tip of his tongue sought entrance as his thigh nudged between hers. Elizabeth gently sipped at the velvet thrust, encouraging further exploration. Groaning deep in his throat, he rubbed his upper thigh gently at the juncture of her legs.

No one had ever touched the passionate part of her being with such longing. A laughing question usually quelled an overly ardent male. She had never felt less inclined to laugh. Awareness stretched from his point of contact, over taut breasts, to her lips. Her hands freed his shirt from the waistband of his beltless slacks.

His shoulders were smooth and taut, as she had imagined. Gliding her fingers up his spine, over the muscles covering his shoulder blades, she drew him deeper into the contours of her mouth. Long fingernails dug into his back as he pressed harder against her; she sighed with pleasure at the sensations he aroused, and pulled him even closer.

"Lord, woman, who would believe you could

feel better than you look?" His fingers threaded through her hair, fanning it over the whiteness of his pillow.

With unerring precision, he unbuttoned the prim, tailored blouse, and unsnapped the front bra clip. Strong, long fingers kneaded the firm, round globes as his tongue dove again into the honeyed sweetness of her mouth. The tip circled, swirled, then plunged, over and over.

Skin afire, she knew the movements of his mouth indicated a growing passion far beyond stopping or controlling. He wanted her intimately. Twisting, arching closer, she also knew she did not want to stop the probing, thrusting, stroking man she held so closely.

Uninhibited, as eager to explore as he obviously was, she discovered his flat nipples were as sensitive as her own. Moving her inner thigh against his upper leg, trapping it, excited him, and he increased the pace of the rubbing motion.

As his lips left hers and moved to the peaks of her breasts, he rolled the taut point between his tongue and the roof of his mouth. Fingers beneath the short hairs at the nape of his neck, she held his head closer as his lips and teeth teased both breasts. Expertly his hands had brought the twin globes together. Moist lips moved from one to the other, neglecting neither. She felt as though they would burst as his teeth nibbled, lips caressed, and hands kneaded. All thought of turning back fled. The forbidden fruit was hers.

Kissing his brow, hair, and ears, she feverishly encouraged his lovemaking by whispering his name.

"Jared, give me more . . . more."

She sought relief from the building pressure. Her body arched against his, signaling the ache within. Jared raked whiskers against her breasts, branding them as his. Deserting the throbbing, pulsating peaks, he returned to her swollen lips, gliding into their welcoming opening.

One hand gently slid under the elasticized band of her skirt, slip, and panty hose, and eased them to her knees. Then with one swift motion she was nude from the waist down.

Sipping at his tongue, she arched her hips, not wanting the stroking rhythm of their straining bodies to stop. His caress answered her demand; the tempo grew faster. The exquisite torture caused by the questing lips and gentle strokes brought her nerve endings from beneath her skin, exposing them to the inconceivable pleasure.

The sound of her name being repeated in short gasps with a questioning lilt made her beg in answer, "Please, please, make love to me."

Without breaking intimate contact, he shed his clothes. Elizabeth's eyes eagerly rounded as she discovered what had been hidden. Straddling her, he slowly eased his large manhood within her.

Eyes closed, she gloried at his infinitely slow

thrust. Silky smooth legs wrapped around his waist.

"Elizabeth," he groaned. "Oh, God, you're so warm, so wonderful. Trapping me . . . enslaving me."

With circular, lifting motions, they traveled into the Garden of Eden. Jared's voice led her on, calling her name, telling her what he wanted, needed. Frantically her lower body twisted, arched, plunged, then exploded as the final height of passion was reached. Her fingers clutched his buttocks, staying at the exploding peak, savoring its height. A rush of warmth filled her as Jared shuddered. The journey of love was complete.

Above her, his hands moved over her waist, navel, and breasts. Carefully, tenderly, she was brought back to earth.

"You turn my blood to molten gold," he whispered. "I'll never have enough of you."

She stared at the man she knew she loved. A tear of joy slid from the corner of one dark-brown orb. Jared licked the jewel as it slid toward her ear. Circling the shell-like orfice with the tip of his tongue while his breathing returned to normal, he moved to her side.

"It was wonderful," she murmured before capturing his parted lips. Softly they joined with hers. The tenderness of her body was healed by the sweetness of his kiss. Cradled together, they lay, their passion sated. Lips touching, both drifted into a light sleep.

"You're doing it again." Green eyes sparkled with amusement.

"What?" she asked dreamily.

"Smiling that peculiar smile."

She had been dreaming about the prince in a fairy tale awakening the princess, after one hundred years of sleeping, with a kiss. She had been awakened to unequaled passion by Jared's kisses. *Thank goodness the modern-day prince does more than kiss!*

Snuggling closer, she answered, "I have to keep some secrets from you. Men like mysterious women."

"Mysterious or not, I wanted you from the very beginning," he said while fingering a golden strand of her fiery hair.

"In your office?" she asked, forgetting about being seen at Nino's. A wide grin split his face. Elizabeth thought he was smiling at her comment. "Your office affords enough privacy for a mad, passionate love scene."

The smile broadened.

"What's so funny?" she demanded.

"We all have our little secrets," he answered, trying to pique her interest.

"Oh, you!" she said, pounding his chest playfully. "You're provoking me to get me to divulge my secret."

"If you say so," he agreed. The teasing twinkle shone brightly. "I promise not to be angry when you explain your smile, if you promise not to be angry when I tell you mine," he bargained.

"No deal."

How could she reveal the fact he had been the object of innumerable fantasies. His head would be so big, he'd have to squeeze it together to get through the bedroom door.

"We'll bargain again after I've fed you. I don't want your stomach to growl at me again."

Thumb and forefinger tweaked a hair on his chest.

"That's for leading me on at lunchtime and not even kissing me."

Grabbing her fingers, he extended her arm overhead and slipped his lips to the nearest breast. Between nibbles he said, "I promised . . . myself . . . not . . . to touch . . . you . . . unless . . . you asked." He nipped the erect rosy point. "You did ask."

"Like a baby asking for candy." Slowly she trailed her free hand down through dark, curly chest hairs, over his stomach, and lower. Jared stiffened as her fingers wove toward their objective. "And, childlike, I savored every morsel," she concluded, flexing her fingers.

"Honey, you'd better stop or you'll get more than you bargained for. You're driving me wild." He groaned as she again teased him with her fingers. "Again?"

"Yes. Slowly. Tenderly."

He answered her request with actions, not words. Without the frantic need of their first mating, he stroked and soothed and stroked and soothed again. The words of love he spoke took her higher than their first journey. As she reached the golden heights of the sun, it burst, spreading fiery meteors in all directions.

Later, a grin on both their faces, they sat across from each other and satisfied their gastronomic appetites in a companionable silence, broken only by the strains of music from the stereo.

I'd sleep on a bed of four-inch nails if you were beside me, she thought. Nothing had prepared her for the breathing fire that had enveloped and consumed her. As she chewed a small piece of pork chop, her lips curved farther upward. *I guess all women feel the same way about the man they love.*

"Maybe you answered the right ad after all."

His words wiped away the smile. As her lips drooped, she pushed the food around her plate. When she looked up, she saw Jared hiding his mouth behind his napkin, but heard his chuckle.

"Not funny, Mr. McKnight."

"I couldn't help it." He replaced the napkin on his lap. "It certainly removed that complacent, secretive smile. Besides, you know I have other plans for your delightfully sexy body." The words were a blend of mirth and seduction.

"What plans?"

Marriage? Would she accept? Is a forty-pound robin fat if he ain't long?

"Care to bargain again?"

"No deal."

Frustrated at his unwillingness to make any

declaration of love, she shoved a piece of meat through the gravy and under the rice. Her throat constricted as the words declaring her love stuck in her throat, unable to get past her tongue and teeth . . . and pride.

Attuned to her discomfort, Jared changed the subject by asking about the plans for Saturday. Enthusiastically she told him about the arrangements that had been made. A mysterious smile fixed his features as she rambled on and on. When she wound down, he asked her what she thought of his sister. As she relayed her unfounded fears at meeting Ms. McKnight, he roared with laughter.

Dinner was concluded over coffee and brandy served in the living room. They sat side by side on the down-filled leather couch. His arm was draped casually over her shoulder, holding her lightly. Jared was relaxed, telling delightful, amusing stories about Mary and himself growing up. The scrapes and fights they had been in made Elizabeth wish she had not been an only child.

"How many crumb crunchers do you want?"

"At least two," she responded. "I'd like twins."

"They don't run in my family. Are there twins in yours?"

"None I know of," she answered, a gleam of hope flaring at the comparison of family lineage. "We'd better clean up the kitchen," she muttered, not wanting cold water splashed on their conversation.

Yawning, Jared said, "Skip the dishes. Let's take a nap."

Seeing the wicked glint in his eye, she knew if they took a quick nap she'd never leave the warmth of his bed. Silently she shook her head.

Flaunting her new love life by staying the night rubbed against her grain. This was their own special memory. She didn't want it exposed to anyone. The taste of forbidden fruit was as golden and delicious as the apple, but indescribable.

Standing in front of her apartment door, Jared wrapped his arms around her shoulder and said, "I have to go to Dallas tomorrow. Are you going with me?"

"I'd love to, but there are a million and one things to do before Saturday."

"Dedication and loyalty so soon?" he teased.

"I thought this reception was important to you?" She evaded answering by returning a question.

"It is, but I want you with me."

"I can't be in two places at once."

Elizabeth could see by the expression on his face that Jared had some inner conflict running through his thoughts.

"I have to go to Dallas."

"And I have work to do here."

Their voices lowered, creating an intimate circle.

"Stalemate." Jared grimaced, obviously disliking being thwarted. "Miss me?"

"I'll miss you five minutes from now," she replied honestly.

Their lips brushed. Tightening his hold, Jared parted her lips, coaxing a deeper response. His arms seemed to pull her inside his body, allowing them to be one. Withdrawing, she saw Jared's green eyes become smoky.

"I'll be back," he said huskily, the words slipping from his lips into hers.

Punching her pillow for the hundredth time, Elizabeth tried to quiet her thoughts and get to sleep. Their lovemaking had been exquisite, but now that they were apart, doubts entered, causing havoc.

Had the tune she had been singing been an open invitation? She had no inkling of how he felt other than he wanted her. Would passion be enough? Wouldn't living with Jared on a casual basis result in more pain in the long run than the fleeting happiness she would have? An affair could be more captivating and emotionally crippling than anything she cared to experience.

The problem was further complicated by her working for Gems Unlimited. She knew the office grapevine would carry any news of whom the boss was currently dating. Seeing and being with him daily would quietly drive her insane if their passion dwindled.

With a loud thump she cursed her introspection. Dissecting his motives was turning the beauty of their lovemaking into merely a lustful coupling. *Stop it*, her mind shrieked, then condemned, *why did you fall into his bed!* All of these self-doubts could have been avoided had she been in control of her emotions. Any further involvement would complicate the situation even more. Acceptance of that single fact left only one distasteful choice.

CHAPTER SEVEN

"I really appreciate your going with me," Elizabeth said, addressing Mary.

"My pleasure. Planning a reception in a house you've never seen is difficult. I'm surprised big brother isn't your guide."

Mary remained by the door as Elizabeth gathered a notebook and purse from the bottom drawer of her desk.

"Jared's in Dallas."

"Business before pleasure? Or is he on the run?" Mary raised one dark brow.

Shrugging her shoulders, Elizabeth didn't answer. She couldn't answer. Seeds of doubt made the words another dark shadow on their relationship.

Both women left the office building and entered Elizabeth's car content with thoughtful silence.

"Are you falling in love with Jared?" Mary asked as she closed the car door.

Elizabeth paused before inserting the ignition key. "You don't beat around the bush, do you?"

"Not when a direct question avoids confusion." Mary twisted in the seat, turning toward Elizabeth with a pensive stare. Jaw set, she was determined to get an answer.

Turning the ignition with a flick of the wrist, Elizabeth brought the powerful car to life. Checking the rearview mirror, then signaling, she pulled the car into the slow-moving traffic.

"Yes, but since I haven't told him, I was reluctant to tell you."

"Thank God!" Jared's sister replied, obviously relieved. "He's been disappointed too many times. You two may have started out on the wrong foot, but all of the misunderstandings are cleared up, aren't they?"

"More or less." She had no intention of revealing how intimate they were or the problems caused by their involvement.

"Good. I haven't seen Jared this excited about a girl since he was a teenager. I advised to forget about any past hurts and go for it."

"What do you mean?"

"Women have been more interested in Jared's money than in the man. Being a member of the nouveau riche isn't easy."

"How do you know I'm not one of those women?"

"Your apparent relief when I told you I was his sister, for one, intuition for the other. Am I wrong?"

"I don't need Jared's money. Wealth and position aren't strangers to me." Smiling, she glanced at Mary, then said, "Must be the man."

"Think you can get through the barriers he's put up?" Mary asked.

"What barriers?"

"Well," Mary paused. "He hides behind a corporate mask. The logic of the business world is much easier to trust than illogical emotions."

"Are you saying he used Dallas as an excuse to get away from me?" Disbelief registered as the pitch of her voice rose.

Mary considered the question thoughtfully. Twin horizontal lines faintly etched her forehead. "I've known about the Dallas deal, so probably he didn't consciously plan an escape route. However, he will probably be awfully 'busy' even though you're next door."

Elizabeth recalled asking him to take her to lunch. He had been busy then. Had he been trying to avoid an emotional entanglement when he refused? Had their physical attraction made him invite her to fix dinner? He'd issued the invitation after refraining from kissing her, hadn't he? Mary was right. He was afraid of emotional involvement.

"The barriers are still in place. Any sugges-

122

tions for getting around, over, under, or through them?" Elizabeth asked.

Laughing, Mary replied, "Hang in there. Knowing the tactics and the reasons behind them should strengthen your arsenal of feminine weapons."

Nodding her head in agreement, Elizabeth went on. "What was he like growing up?"

"Mischievous. Studious. Independent. Protector of his tag-a-long sister. I idolized him, and he knew it. When he turned eighteen and worked full-time while attending night school, I was lost. The void wasn't filled until I met and married Steve." Her mouth clamped shut, sealing any further confidences behind her lips.

"And . . ." Elizabeth prompted. She could see Mary mentally closing the door to any private confidences, but felt she too needed a sympathetic ear.

"And when Jared needed extra help to run the business, I volunteered. Steve didn't relish the idea of playing second fiddle to Gems Unlimited or to Jared. After tolerating late meals, a messy house, and an exhausted wife, he walked out." A deep sigh ended the revelation. The hand that had covered the lower portion of her face now was clenched in her lap. She splayed her fingers, trying to let the tension run out of the ends.

"At first the McKnight pride kept me from changing anything." Mary pulled the polish off one chipped nail. "Now I'm determined to correct my mistakes." With a sardonic smile, she

123

confided, "I'd shovel a hole and stand in it, just to kiss his feet."

Eyes on the road, Elizabeth flashed a grin at her companion. Immaculate, self-assured businesswomen rarely admit to groveling for a man.

"One lesson I've learned the hard way. Love is like a bank account," Mary philosophized, "if you put love in, it's returned with interest. If you constantly deplete your reserves, you end up with a pink slip with Overdrawn in bold letters. I've had three months to become a saver rather than a spender." Her jaw tightened, her intent clear.

"Sorry, Elizabeth. I didn't intend to burden you with my problems, but you're a good listener. I needed to say the words out loud."

"Which way?" Elizabeth asked when she had reached the turning point in Mary's directions.

"Left on Chapel Road. Third house on the right," Mary directed absentmindedly, her thoughts still on Steve.

Slowing the car, Elizabeth turned on Chapel. Tall pine trees and manicured lawns graced the yards of the homes. Each house was set on three to five acres, she approximated. At the third mailbox she steered the car into the curved drive. Azalea bushes lined the road leading to the spacious, contemporary dwelling. Multiflora rosebushes bloomed profusely against the brick and cedar walls. Long, undraped windows, two stories in height, beckoned.

Upon leaving the car, the odor from the decorative bushes enveloped Elizabeth. As she turned back to wait for Mary, her keen ears heard the soft whispering of pine needles rustling in the light breeze.

Key in hand, Mary advanced up the brick path.

"Welcome to Pinerose." Stepping around Elizabeth, she opened the door, extending her arm, which allowed Elizabeth to cross the threshold first.

Elizabeth gasped at the visual delight the interior provided. An eclectic blend of modern and antique furniture bathed in sunlight from the tall windows surrounding the room gave the impression of being in a clearing amid a forest of pines. Hanging baskets of ferns, impatiens, and airplane plants heightened the effect.

"It's gorgeous," Elizabeth exclaimed as her eyes moved from one corner of the room to the other. Catching a glimmer of sparkling blue, she walked to the back of the house. Nestled in the trees was a swimming pool resembling a small pond. The flagstone coping on the edge of the pool and the small waterfall that tumbled into the shallow end of the pool completed the illusion.

"It's as though we're in a little piece of heaven," she revered.

"Thanks," Mary said. "It's a shame no one lives here now. After Dad's heart attack, Mom insisted they move to west Texas, where they both grew up. This place is special to all of us."

"You mean it sits empty? Who takes care of it?"

"A housekeeper," she answered flatly. "Jared lived here until a year ago. The folks could sell it and make a fantastic profit, but . . . it's the first nice home they owned, and they're reluctant to part with it."

Elizabeth understood. Others might consider it foolish, or a waste of money, but sentimentality doesn't have a price tag. She knew her father would rather lose his arm than the watch he wore.

Her thoughts were interrupted when Mary said pointedly, "Jared would probably want to live here, should he marry."

Elizabeth assimilated the statement, but refused to comment on the possibility of living in Jared's family home. It would be presumptuous, but the flicker of a fantasy edged the back of her mind nonetheless. A miniature Jared and Elizabeth scampering through the woods, splashing in the pool, enjoying childhood and teenage parties with proud parents blissfully standing in the background momentarily passed in front of her eyes. *Stop it*, she reprimanded herself. Her love was a one-way street which did not lead to Chapel Road.

"Where do you live?" she asked, avoiding any more flights of the imagination.

"Steve and I have our own place down the road. I'd like to stop there before we drive back."

Both women sat at the dinette table overlooking the pool and began making final plans for the reception. Elizabeth extracted the small notebook from her purse and began making a sketch of the pool area. The caterer had suggested serving the buffet outside, as they had on a previous occasion.

The morning passed swiftly as Mary told about parties the McKnights had held in their home. Elizabeth made copious notes. She wanted this reception to meet the standards Mary's family would expect. Fortunately the housekeeper planned to be available to help the caterers set up. Competent help was a vital necessity.

Having discussed the preliminary plans Elizabeth had made, Mary went over the guest list in detail and told her to invite a couple of her friends if she wanted to. Invitations had been sent the moment they had been received from the card shop. It was late notice for a weekend gathering, but Mary was certain most of the people invited would come. Her parents visited Houston so infrequently, their friends welcomed any occasion to see them.

On their return trip to Houston, Elizabeth felt a sisterly closeness to Mary. Mary showed her own home with great pride. The feeling of warmth and love was evident as Jared's sister walked through telling stories about the knick-knacks she and Steve had collected over the years.

As they shared opinions about furniture and decorations, they entered a small room next to the master suite. Sunny yellow paper in a child's print surprised Elizabeth. A crib was placed near a window shaded by pines. Her eyes widened as she turned to Mary.

"Yes, I am," Mary said, answering Elizabeth's silent question. Mary touched her slightly rounded stomach. "If all else fails, which I hope it won't, I'll tell Steve about the baby." A maternal pride glowed as she touched the small chest of drawers. "We had given up hope. I guess I had to grow up before becoming a mother," she said with a rueful smile.

Hugging Mary, Elizabeth reassured her, "You'll be a wonderful mother."

Mary dozed quietly on their return trip, lulled by the hum of the engine. Elizabeth's thoughts centered around the sleeping woman. Although Mary had told her how important the reception was for the whole family, she still did not understand why. And what was troubling Mary so? Could it be Steve and Jared had crossed swords? Maybe she could help by keeping Jared occupied until Mary had an opportunity to smooth the choppy waters.

Mary's help had certainly been invaluable. Now she understood a few of the baffling characteristics Jared had displayed. She also knew Jared had reasons for being wary of any permanent relationship. The doubts and fears she had faced the night before were not resolved, but they had been clarified.

Mary awoke. Stretching her cramped legs, she apologized for being such poor company.

"Expectant mothers need their rest," Elizabeth said, grinning as she climbed out of the car.

"Elizabeth." Mary's hand touching her upper

arm stopped Elizabeth before entering the building. "I resigned today. My replacement is taking over tomorrow. I thought I'd better warn you in case Jared snaps your head off." Mary shrugged her shoulders. With a broad wink she added, "This mother hen is going home to feather her nest."

Elizabeth watched with mixed emotions as the young pregnant woman skipped away, dodging other pedestrians. Her laughter lingered when her presence was gone.

Roses. Dozens and dozens of roses. Red, yellow, white, and pink blossoms crowded Elizabeth's office. A small white envelope perched on a clear plastic stand on her desk. Heart racing, she swept past the rose-filled vases, plucking the card from its holder.

Dial 003. I'll be gone until Friday. Dinner at 7:00. Three for yes. Two for no.

He wants me to grunt over the phone? No way. Dialing 003, she waited as the phone buzzed. A recorder clicked on. Jared's prerecorded voice came through the earpiece.

"Hello, honey. Hope you like roses. When the tone beeps, please say yes. Till Friday?" Beeeeeeeeeeeeeeeep.

Chuckling, Elizabeth placed her lips against the receiver and delivered three loud, smacking kisses.

* * *

Balancing two vases of roses, her purse, and a notebook, Elizabeth struggled to open the lock on her front door.

"Got a match?" she heard from behind her.

"Not since Wonder Woman was discontinued," she quipped in response to Sara's voice.

"Here. Let me help," Sara offered, taking both vases of roses. "Mmm, smell heavenly. They couldn't possibly be from the ogre you work for, could they?"

"Possibly," Elizabeth teased, knowing she was about to receive the third degree.

Inside the apartment Sara placed the flowers on the coffee table and tried to appear as though she were patiently waiting for an explanation, or an invitation to dinner.

"How's the world of high finance coping with Serendipity Sara and No-Sense-of-Humor Crosby?" she inquired while deciding how to avoid Sara's avid interest in her own love life.

"Crosby caught me using a paper clip today instead of a money strap. Big deal. Does he realize how disgusting it is to have him towering over me, barking out reprimands, when all I can see is the inside of his nose?"

Elizabeth laughed. "Oh, the plight of short people," she responded.

"So I cut his tie in half," Sara sputtered, then giggled.

"You what?"

"Cut his tie in half. I'm here to tell you, that brought his nose down. With two inches of tie hanging down from the Windsor knot, and the rest of it flapped over his tie tack, he looked as ridiculous as I felt."

"Are you joining the ranks of the unemployed?"

"Not today. He was so stunned, he pivoted on one giraffe leg and strode to his office. Later I received fifty straps to bundle money with and a handwritten note. He's coming by tonight to collect a new tie."

"Did you buy one?"

"Did I ever." Removing the slender box from underneath her arm, she took off the lid and held the contents up for Elizabeth's inspection. The moonbeam face became rounder as the impish smile became wider at Elizabeth's reaction.

At first glance the tie appeared to be a conservative brown tie with squiggles and tiny blue letters making an overall design. On closer inspection Elizabeth saw the letters were MCP and the blurred design was actually piglets.

In a fit of giggles Elizabeth collapsed on the sofa holding her sides. "If he didn't fire you when you sheared off his tie, he will when you call him a male chauvinist pig!"

Sara shrugged off the probable outcome as unimportant. "Why can't I have a boss who believes in sexual harassment? I'd love it!" With a sly lifting of her lashes, she inquired casually, "How's your boss?"

The ringing of the telephone saved Elizabeth from answering the leading question. Grinning wickedly at Sara, she jumped off the sofa and ran to the phone.

"Hello?"

"Kisses are better than grunts," Jared's husky baritone voice answered.

"Jared! I didn't expect your call." With one hand she waved good-bye to Sara and pointed to the door. "What a lovely surprise," she added with unconcealed delight in her voice.

"My. My. Such nice telephone manners. Can't you talk?" he asked, perceptively aware she might have an audience.

Noting Sara firmly planted in the middle of the living room, and not heading toward the door, she said, "Not here. If you'll hold on, I'll pick up the extension in my bedroom."

"I'll be here," he replied, "but I'd rather be where you're headed."

Casting Sara a baleful glare, Elizabeth said, "It's my boss. Since you can't take a polite hint, would you like to pick up the phone and ask him the questions you're dying to have answered?"

"An MCP at work disguised as a giraffe, and a clam at home disguised as a sex kitten," she complained lightly, crossing to the door. "God made a mistake when he gave me the mind of a stripper and the body of a mobile home."

Knowing Sara had given up too easily, and her penchant for gluing her ear to doors, Elizabeth decided it would still be wise to use the phone in the bedroom.

"Thanks for the flowers," she said after settling on the bed.

"I'd like to give you more than flowers," he suggestively drawled. "I'd like to have you back in my apartment singing to me." His soft laughter sent chills up her spine. She could feel heat traveling from the tips of her toes to the crown of her head. The heat melted her resolve and she felt herself weakening.

"Elizabeth? Are you there?"

"Yes," she replied succinctly, his words leaving her tongue-tied.

"Can't talk and fantasize at the same time?" he teased. Not giving her time to reply, he asked, "Are you missing me?"

"Loyal employees always miss their boss," she said evasively as she stretched out on her bed.

"Not the answer I'm searching for. Try again."

"Yes. I miss you." How she wanted to add, I love you. Of course I miss you.

"It's lonely here. I know you're busy, but would you fly down tomorrow night? Then you can fly back with me the following day. I won't even dock your pay," he teasingly coaxed.

"Are you serious, or are you joking?"

"Both. I know you're too busy, but I want you here with me. Right now."

Winding the phone cord around her finger, she paused before answering. The seductive tone in his voice had caused a prickling sensation along the back of her neck. She imagined him as she was, stretched out, relaxing on a bed.

133

"More cold showers," he muttered, more to himself than to her.

"Do they help?"

Jared laughed, then asked, "Feeling frustrated?"

"Why would I be frustrated, Mr. McKnight?" she asked, purposely lowering the pitch of her voice, making it sultry.

"Why indeed?" She could tell a wide grin had spread over his face as he answered her parry. "I want to be with you badly," he said in earnest. "I need to touch you. Hold you. Make love to you."

Her breasts became taut as she remembered him doing all three. A throbbing sensation below her stomach made her cross her legs. His voice, alone, was causing the flames of desire to lick through her.

"Oh, Jared," she said softly.

"My name sounded the same way after we made love." She heard a muffled groan cross the lines. "Talking on the phone has only added to my frustration. I'll see you Friday night. Okay?" he asked.

"Are you taking me any place special? Do I need to dress up?" she asked in an effort to prolong the conversation.

"I know where I'd prefer to take you. No clothes would be appropriate."

"Jared, be serious."

"Honey, I am serious," he replied dryly.

She didn't answer, but smiled into the mouthpiece.

"You're smiling, aren't you?" he asked.

"Yes."

"Care to explain why?" he prodded.

"Not on the phone. I'm not as uninhibited as you. Friday, maybe," she tempted.

"I could learn to hate leaving Houston. The man I'm buying equipment from doesn't appreciate my daydreaming, or my insisting on describing a fantastic lady named Elizabeth."

"Did you really tell him about me?" she asked, knowing he never let anything interfere with business.

"No. But my tongue is sore from biting it back," he complained with humor.

"Poor darling. Shall I kiss it all better?"

"I'll count on it!" he responded. "I'd call tomorrow, but I can't afford the cold-water bill the hotel tacked on for excessive use. I'll see you Friday," he said, concluding the conversation.

"Friday," she echoed.

Placing the phone back on the cradle, she sat staring at it. The minutes would pass as slowly as hours between now and his arrival. There was so much to admire and love about the man. He's clever, witty, fun, sexy, handsome. Adjectives could describe, but couldn't reveal the whole man, she mused.

"Hurry up, Friday!"

135

CHAPTER EIGHT

Thursday whirled by. Elizabeth checked the rental agencies and confirmed the delivery of silver, china, and linens. She spent an hour with the florist choosing the cut flowers that would decorate the living room, kitchen, and the buffet table, as well as miniature arrangements to be placed in the downstairs bathrooms.

When she wasn't making calls, she was receiving them from couples accepting the invitation. Mary telephoned, reminding her to invite any friends of her own to the reception. By five o'clock she felt as though she had been shoved through a knothole backward.

Opening the apartment door, her main thought centered around a long, hot, soothing bath. Kicking her black lizard heels into the front closet, her nylon-clad toes wriggled into the plush carpet.

A sharp rap, a twist of the doorknob, followed by her father's face peeking around the door nearly scared the wits out of her.

"Dad, you scared me. I thought I was about to be robbed, raped, and pillaged," she exclaimed before giving him a welcome-home hug.

"You need to lock your door," he answered sternly before returning the squeeze.

"When did you get in?"

"Midafternoon. I talked to Sara at the bank and she told me about your connection with Gems Unlimited. I decided I couldn't wait to find out how you relented and are allowing your designs to be mass-produced, so . . . here I am."

"Your brilliant daughter is creating divine pieces of jewelry and is dating the boss, Jared McKnight." She stressed key words, hoping to discourage any pointed questioning.

Gesturing toward the bar with one hand, he asked, "Should we celebrate?"

"Nothing specific to celebrate, but I'll make you one of my famous Texas margaritas if you like." Moving behind the bar, she emptied an ice tray into the blender and began measuring out the ingredients.

"Tell me about Jared McKnight," he said, searching her eyes for hidden clues.

Not wanting her father to know she had literally fallen into his bed on short acquaintanceship, she ducked down below the cabinet, pretending to search for the tequila and triple sec.

"It's on the counter. Come back up here."

Raising slowly, she said sincerely, "I love him. What more can I say?"

"Your face is in direct competition with the pink in your blouse. Want to tell me more?" The smile signaled he wouldn't pry in any direction she wasn't willing to take.

"You'll meet him Saturday."

Carefully she measured one shot of tequila, one shot of triple sec, and one shot of fresh lime juice. Blending the ingredients with a glass stirrer, she used her index finger to dab triple sec around the edge of the glass. *Not too sanitary*, she thought, *but the booze would kill any germs.* She pulled special coarse salt, kept in a plastic container to keep the humidity out, off a glass shelf. With a twisting motion she swirled the damp rim in the salt. Elizabeth filled the stemmed glass with cracked ice, then poured in the light green mixture. One quick stir chilled the beverage.

"Mmm. Texas perfection," George said after tasting the cool drink. Picking up the stirrer, he slowly chased the ice around the rim of the glass. "What's the big event Saturday?"

"A reception. Jared officially takes over the reins of the company, and unofficially his sister, Mary, is going to recapture her husband."

"Sounds interesting. Any other unofficial capturing planned?" He smiled wickedly.

"Not unless *you* have some deep dark secret

you're going to reveal." Elizabeth diverted the conversation back to him and away from herself.

"Elusive little brat, aren't you? What happened to the sweet young girl who used to tell her daddy everything?" George swiveled around on the barstool as if looking for the missing child.

"She grew up. Maybe her daddy needs to fall in love again."

"Whoa! Don't start playing cupid for your old man. Why do I have the feeling you're trying to get me off your trail by harping on my love life?"

The doorbell rang. Excusing herself, she walked gracefully across the living room and opened the door.

"Hello, love." Jared's voice rumbled from deep in his chest. "I came back early—" Stopping in mid-sentence, he glared at George.

Before Elizabeth could introduce either man, Jared barged through the opening, and stood towering over George.

"I can see I should have called before coming over, Elizabeth," Jared said harshly, his eyes never leaving George's face. "Funny—I actually thought you might be lonely."

George stepped back with a controlled smile. "Now, just a minute, son. There's no need to talk to my daughter in that tone of voice."

Jared moved toward him, pointing an accusing finger at his chest. "I'll use any tone of voice I want with . . ."

"Jared! Dad!" Elizabeth placed herself between them.

"Your daughter?" Jared asked, dropping his hand.

"Yes!" Elizabeth shouted.

"I thought . . ." Jared began, blushing as he finally recognized George from the night he'd first seen Elizabeth.

"It's rather obvious what you thought," George broke in, extending one open hand.

With a jerky motion Jared captured the hand of friendship and pumped it zealously. Then, becoming aware of his crushing hold, he loosened it abruptly.

"Sorry about that," Jared said, instantly contrite and terribly embarrassed.

George grinned forgivingly. "Me too. Apology accepted." Turning toward his daughter, he added, "I think your young man would like to take you out. Why don't you run along and change. We'll get acquainted in your absence."

Her vision Ping-Ponged from Jared to her father.

"Do as you're told," Jared added gruffly.

Mumbling something about being dismissed like a naughty five-year-old, Elizabeth spun around and left the room, silently fuming as she slammed the bedroom door. Men! First they're about to duke it out; then they unanimously order their savior from the room. She could hear deep laughter from the opposite side of the door.

"Elizabeth eavesdrops. Why don't we talk quietly in the kitchen," she overheard her father say.

Now he's telling my secrets! Next he'll be getting out

the bare-baby-in-the-bathtub pictures! Elizabeth entered the walk-in closet. Instantly she spied the slinky dress she had worn on their first date. Being a vamp was a role preferable to being cast as a child.

Light tapping at the door accompanied Sara's voice asking to come in.

Frustrated, Elizabeth yelled, "Come in."

"Elizabeth? What are your dad and Jared doing in the kitchen, whispering?"

"The mighty warriors are holding a council meeting and sent the squaw to her teepee." She shook her fists at the ceiling. Placing her hands on her hips, spreading her feet apart, she looked ready to take on both of them.

Sara laughed, reading her stance. "I'll put my money on you, hon. They don't have a prayer!"

Sense of humor prevailing over anger, Elizabeth's frown smoothed as her lips twitched. Within moments they both were howling with laughter.

"You should have . . . seen Jared . . ." Elizabeth said between bursts of mirth. ". . . pointing that accusing finger at Dad. Jared thought he was protecting me from a lecherous old man."

Peals of laughter burst forth at the absurdity.

"God, that's funny. Jared defending your honor against your father." Sara clutched the bedspread as another spasm of giggles racked her body. "I love it!"

Sara levered herself off the mattress, wiped her eyes, and said, "You're not going to let them get

141

away with it, are you?" The devilish twinkle Elizabeth was used to seeing in Sara's eyes when she was hatching a plot was burning brightly. "Can I help you dress for the occasion?"

With a nod the mischievous gleam in her own dark eyes made them almost black. Whipping off her business suit, she vowed to have the last laugh. Quickly she donned the clothing Sara laid out: a pair of faded jeans, a T-shirt emblazed with SOMEONE IN TEXAS LOVES ME, and dirty sneakers. Seated in front of the vanity mirror she watched as Sara braided her long hair into two pigtails. With a wide grin Elizabeth added the final touch: two large red bows. She was transformed into a well-developed, shiny-faced, ten-year-old as she entered the kitchen.

Jared's back was toward the entrance. George glanced up, saw the outfit, and laughed heartily at his daughter's sauciness. Jerking his head around, Jared's mouth dropped before he slapped his thigh and joined in on the guffaws.

"Be careful, Jared. She's a sassy thing," George testified.

Reaching around her waist, Jared pulled the recalcitrant woman onto his lap.

"Jeans . . . okay. T-shirt . . . okay. Pigtails . . . NO WAY." He jerked out the decorative bows, ran his fingers through the plaits and separated the coils. Winking at George, he jibed, "Will I still look like a cradle-robber?" Jared stood, dumping Elizabeth on her feet. "George, it's been a pleasure."

142

"Same here, Jared." Again the older man offered his hand. "This time try not to break all the small bones."

After shaking hands George slapped Jared on the back in the age-old masculine gesture of friendship. Cocking his head toward his daughter, he said, "Curb her temper, gets her into trouble all the time."

Lacing his fingers with Elizabeth's, Jared tugged her toward the door. Masterfully, for her father's benefit, he commanded, "Come on, woman. You have three bad marks on your report card. Punishment is just around the corner." The broad smile and bright green eyes reassured George that any punishment would be mutually enjoyable.

They were only a few steps past the building when Jared halted their progress to the car. In broad daylight, with traffic streaming down the street, he lifted her and claimed her lips in a hard, hungry kiss.

Forgetting her anger, Elizabeth immediately responded, locking her arms around his shoulders. She clung and hung limply against the man she loved. If his phone call had weakened her will, his kiss had destroyed it.

"That erases one bad mark," he whispered into her ear.

"If that's my punishment, I'm a masochist. Punish me some more," she whispered in return.

Releasing her slowly, Jared lightly held their hips together.

143

"Hungry?" he asked.

With the slightest of rotation, she answered, "Starving!"

"Wanton baggage."

"Sex fiend."

Drawing her closer, he blew gently into her ear, then nibbled at the small lobe. "You're back up to three bad marks."

The danger of being seduced on a busy street in the six o'clock traffic made her heart race. "We're stopping traffic," she said sweetly.

Honking horns blared as the occupants of the cars rubbernecked. A construction worker wearing a hardhat shouted, "Hey, bud. Everybody loves a lover . . . except in the rush hour."

Protecting her from curious eyes, Jared twisted her under his shoulder and matched her short strides to his car. Once in the car, Elizabeth felt his hand run from knee to thigh and back again. His leg muscles flexed when she echoed his action. Capturing her hand, he squeezed it.

"I'm starved. Shall we eat at Tony's? Rudy's?" he asked, naming two of the plush restaurants in Houston. "Had you dressed properly, I'd have taken you there."

Steering into a well-known drive-in restaurant, he ordered a Kiddie Meal for Elizabeth and two sandwiches, French fries, and a milk shake for himself.

"Jaaarrred!" She strung out the middle letters in his name. "I'm hungry too. A Kiddie Meal isn't enough."

"You cheated me out of a steak dinner with your teeny-bopper costume. You have to pay a forfeit or go hungry." Before he could get the words over his lips, a wide grin split his face.

"You silly devil. Order more for me," she pleaded prettily.

"Silly devil?" he asked, refusing to order.

"Handsome devil!" Elizabeth compromised.

"Make that four cheeseburgers, two fries, and two chocolate milk shakes."

Rolling forward, he braked in front of the drive-up window. After he paid, he received three white bags.

"Wherever we're going, if you want your milk shake thick, you'd better hurry."

Extracting a long, hot, golden French fry, Elizabeth slid it over Jared's lips, then popped it into her mouth.

"Cruel, cruel woman. Here I skip meals, catch the last flight out, and you refuse to share the French fries." In a plaintive voice he tried to make her feel guilty at the injustice of her behavior.

She withdrew another aromatic potato. "Why, Jared. All you need to do is ask . . . nicely."

"Elizabeth!"

"Jared?"

"Please?"

"Open wide," she said as she poked the slender potato into his mouth. Jared licked the fingers, causing little explosions to run up her arm.

145

"Salty." Glancing at her smiling lips, he added, "Sweet."

The doubts that had brutalized her vanished. Being with him wiped them away in one fell swoop. She felt fantastic. The man she loved was beside her. As she fed him one fry at a time her eyes soaked in his handsome ruggedness. Jared was perfect, a perfect male specimen, a perfect lover. The firm lips touching her fingertips brought back the depth of her response less than forty-eight hours ago. Hadn't she known and loved him all her life? In a past life? For all eternity?

She remembered his gentle stroking caresses and relished the memory. A small fire was beginning to kindle from the hot coals still glowing deep within. Closing her eyes, tiny flames began scorching her skin. She envisioned not only the touching, but also the whispered words of encouragement. Each erotic word fanned the flames. She envisioned Jared as he whispered new words of love. Each erotic calling of her name increased her desire. A light film of perspiration broke out on her forehead.

A blast of air-conditioning snapped her back to reality. Fingertips had directed the vent directly on her face.

"Comfortable now? You looked hot."

Hot. Burning. On fire, but not from the sun. She turned toward the window to conceal her burning cheeks. Wanton hussy is right, she chastized herself. Chewing on her inner lip, she tried to bring her physical needs back into control. Was Jared aware of her fantasies? Composing her features, she turned, seeking an answer.

He appeared to be locked in his own mental battle. Lines of strain creased his brow and firm lips were tightened into a thin line.

A minuscule crystal of salt clung to the corner of his lip. Elizabeth removed it with a flick of her tongue. The unexpected intimacy caused Jared to jerk his head toward her. The pink tip grazed the sealed lips briefly.

"Go sit by the door," he ordered, his voice catching. The groove in his cheek deepened as he smiled. "We're nearly there. Don't make me have an accident." Pausing again, he instructed, "You can talk, but don't touch."

She slid away, but her mouth was too dry to talk. The flames and salt had burned away any moisture. Anticipation had strung her nerves tighter than a piano wire. The waiting and wondering during his absence had her emotions silently screaming for relief. She drummed her fingers on the upholstery impatiently. *Damn it, drive faster,* she thought.

CHAPTER NINE

When they passed the Houston Medical Center, Elizabeth guessed their destination. Hermann Park with its live oak trees dripping with Spanish moss would provide shade from the Texas sun. Jared turned left by the Burke Baker Planetarium and headed into the park.

"Bring the dinner. I'll get blankets from the trunk," he ordered after parking the car.

Not waiting, Elizabeth jumped from the car and raced to a picnic table. She hadn't been to the park in years. She watched Jared's long, lithe strides as he strolled toward her. Having discarded his suit jacket and rolled up the sleeves of his pale double-knit shirt, he had changed from business executive to casual date.

Elizabeth watched the muscles across his shoulders as he spread two stadium blankets over the thick St. Augustine grass. She noticed he had first checked to make certain no fire-ant mounds were in the vicinity. Her fingertips were, once again, itching to touch the manmade fibers clinging snugly to his chest. Unconsciously they lightly stroked the fleshy part of her thumb.

"See something you like?" Jared teased lightly.

Holding the bags out, she answered, "Yes. Food." The milk shakes have probably turned into hot chocolate, she thought as she kneeled down and began unpacking their dinner.

"Sure you're only interested in food?"

"Egotist," she replied, keeping her head down and her fingers busy. The slight tremble as she took the lids off their drinks betrayed her flip answer.

"You're racking up the bad marks. Payoff time," he said as he checked the position of the sun, "is about three hours away."

"I'll look forward to it," she responded cheekily.

They sat Indian-style, consuming the contents of the bags. The heat and humidity dropped a few degrees as a northern breeze blew through the oaks. Squirrels scampered up and down the huge tree trunks, acorns clamped between strong jaws.

Replete, Jared lay back with his hands behind his head. Long legs crossed at the ankles completed the relaxed picture. After packing the sandwich wrappers back into the bag, Elizabeth strode to the trash container and disposed of the bundle. Buzzing flies swooshed out as the bags thumped the bottom of the barrel.

"You guys eat here," she told them firmly.

Returning to the blankets, she stood over Jared, letting her eyes drink in his reposing form. Green eyes were closed. Thick dark lashes caused faint shadows beneath his eyes. Or was that exhaustion? She stretched out beside him, wanting to snuggle close to his side, but hesitated, unwilling to awaken him.

"Do you always talk to trash cans?" Jared drawled lazily, peeking out at her from half-closed lids.

"No. But my major in college was fly gibberish," she responded, moving closer.

Chuckling quietly, Jared unfolded one arm and drew her close, making his shoulder a pillow for her head. A gust of wind blew golden-red hair across his face. The long strands brushed against his long lashes and between his lips. Before she pulled them away, his lips pursed, almost refusing to let them escape.

A mixture of Brut and male perspiration mingled in her nose. His arm slackened its hold as his breathing became slow and even. Elizabeth allowed herself to feast on his features. Sleep wiped away the lines of strain and exhaustion. Two faint lines remained across his brow. Lips parted slightly, she could hear a light snore. Grinning, she thought, *He probably snores as loud as a freight train when he's deep in sleep.* For some unknown reason the flaw pleased her.

Three buttons were open, exposing a thick mat of dark, curly hair. She wanted to touch the skin beneath, but refrained. Gently, watching his eyes to make certain her movements did not awaken him, she unbuttoned the remaining buttons. She told herself she had to stop before totally undressing him.

Damn it, Jared, why do I have this intense desire to unclothe you?

Sighing at her own impatience, she laid back in the crook of his arm. The white cumulus clouds drifted overhead, blocking out the direct rays of the sun. She played the childhood game of making objects out of their shapes to pass the time. After sighting a dog, a tailless rat, and an upright vacuum cleaner, her eyes shut and she drifted into sleep.

Swatting a pesky fly away from her nose, Elizabeth drowsily twisted around. Pleasant dreams of Jared brought a smile to her lips. Twitching her nose didn't remove the irksome creature. With one fingertip, her eyes shut, she rubbed at the tickling sensation as it crossed over her nose again. It continued, making tracks over her cheekbone. Slow to awaken, she willed her eyelids up.

Hovering over her, a lock of hair between her thumb and forefinger, Jared trailed the ends over her chin.

"Pesky beast," she muttered, stilling his hand with her own. The milk shake she had drunk earlier made her mouth dry. As she licked her lower lip, she tasted the chocolate.

"Let me."

One eyelid rose marginally. Through reddish-brown lashes she watched his head as it blotted out the graying clouds above them.

The point of his tongue tasted the sweetness, making small currents of electricity charge through her. Elizabeth could feel her heart quicken as his teeth nibbled, pulling at the bow of her lower lip. Warm fingers stroked over her cheek before threading through her hair.

"Chocolate kisses." Jared spoke the words against her lips. Tenderly they met with no urgency. Languidly he spread tiny kisses on her eyes, forehead, chin, and throat. Elizabeth responded, planting butterfly kisses of her own brand. The unshaven cheeks lightly scraped the sensitive skin of her throat.

Elizabeth ran the fleshy part of her palm from his collarbone to waistband. Wanting more than the feather kisses, she tugged his shirt out of his trousers and pulled him closer with her arm. Hair tickled her nose when she kissed his nipple, bringing it erect.

"That's not fair." His hot breath against the flimsy cotton of her T-shirt brought an immediate response, similar to his.

"What's not fair?" she innocently asked, fully aware of the effects her hands were having.

"What you're doing to me."

"What am I doing?" Her fingers went through the dark hair to his other nipple.

Pulling her hips against him intimately, he replied, "That!"

She knew exactly what he meant. Passion glittered from his eyes as he raised his head. Scorching heat emanated from below his waist. His head rising, she glanced around the immediate area and saw it was vacant.

"Don't think . . . feel," Jared demanded as he brought their lips together.

And feel she did. He was a master at synchronizing his hand movements with those of his lips, teeth, and tongue. As his fingers closed over her burgeoning breast, his tongue teased her eager lips. Teasing one swollen rosebud with his fingers, his tongue darted in and out of her mouth. His lips and teeth then nibbled at her earlobe as his fingers lightly pinched the hardening point between his fingertips. The pain of ecstasy raced from her breast to her ear, and raced lower. The empty ache was returning.

Tugging at the crisp hairs on his chest, she inflicted an erotic pain of her own. Her thumb tucked under the back of his belt and traced liquid fire from his spine to below his navel, just under the belt buckle. Stomach muscles tightened in anticipation of unbuckling. Ignoring the physical request, her finger circled his navel. The back of her hand moved between hip bones.

"I want you, Elizabeth," he said, breathing deeply as he spoke. "This isn't enough. Come home with me," he coaxed. His eyes were level with her own. The smoky jade eyes flamed.

Want. Would want get through the barriers she knew he had erected between them? No, she thought, it won't. For her a passing fling wouldn't be enough. All the values she believed in couldn't be shed as easily as their clothing.

Jared lay down, separating their closeness. Covering his eyes with his forearm, he groaned almost inaudibly. Elizabeth touched the dampness on his chest, silently asking forgiveness and understanding for her refusal.

"Don't touch me." Frustration and physical need made the words snarllike.

Flinching as though struck, she moved away. Her own arousal was as acute as his.

"Two minutes," he ground out between clenched jaws, "then I'll be rational."

Sitting up, Elizabeth wrapped her arms around her legs and rocked back and forth. Frustrated by the loss of physical touch and by his rejection at her attempt to placate him, she was miserable.

His fingertips touched her waist.

"It's okay. Stop fretting."

Comforting words slowed the rocking motion. Thoughts were raging a war in her head. This is a man, not a kid, and he's too virile to be celibate. She knew eventually she would have to make a choice. She could know again the joy of physically uniting with him, or she could know the pain of watching him pursue another woman.

Words spilled from her heart in an effort to

stop the direction of her thoughts. "This isn't going to work. It's tearing me up inside."

"It will work," Jared answered tersely.

"It won't."

"Stop arguing," he said as he rolled to his side, propping his head up on his arm.

"I won't be a casual bed partner." Her eyes bore into his as she communicated physically as well as verbally.

"Wait until you've been asked," he responded. The lines on his forehead deepened. "Our problems don't all center around the bed." Reaching over, Jared put his hand on her bent knee to quiet the rocking motion that had begun again. "You're a warm, sensitive, passionate woman. The combination explodes over me like a lit match dropped into a gasoline can—instant combustion."

The knuckles of his hand followed the double stitching on her jeans up to her belt.

"Having been with you makes touching you then holding back impossible," he explained. The warmth radiating from his eyes showed sincerity.

Digesting his words, Elizabeth realized the truth. They had advanced too far to go back ten paces and hold hands. She wanted him every bit as badly as he wanted her. The only difference was the unspoken word . . . love. The problem she understood; the solution was unattainable.

"So? Where do we go from this point?" she asked, wanting him to come up with a solution.

"That depends on you. Tell me exactly what *you* want." Coaxing her, he was asking for the truth.

"I want—" she broke off, unable to tell him she wanted marriage, children, all the things he had never mentioned. "I don't want to be a trinket you admire when it's first spit out of a machine, and then discarded when its surface is scratched." She paused, not wanting to utter the word that had originally brought them together. "I don't want to be your mistress." The dreaded label passed through her lips with the bitterness of arsenic. She hoped that by telling him what she did not want it would clarify what she did want.

"Back to the hands-off policy?" he asked as he pulled up a blade of grass and placed the damp stem into his mouth. "Platonic friends?"

The decision was hers to make. She raised her head to the sky and watched dark thunderclouds rolling in from the north. The wind whipped her hair into disarray.

"Yes."

The monosyllabic answer was accompanied by a flash of lightning and one large drop of rain splashing on her hand. Silently Jared gathered his blanket and waited while she folded hers. Neither spoke as they ran back to the car. Holding the door for her, he tossed both blankets into the back seat. By the time he was in the car, raindrops the size of quarters splattered against the windshield.

Squeezing her eyes shut, Elizabeth sank into

the leather upholstery. Had she given the wrong answer? Why couldn't she settle for less than an ideal love relationship? She had lied again. Forced by pride, she had silenced her tongue from telling the truth. Although lying was abhorrent to her, using her body to bargain for a wedding band was impossible.

The downpour pounded on the roof in hard gusts. The powerful hum of the motor and the windshield wipers swiping off the pouring rain made her intensely aware of the smallness of the car's interior. As the car turned right, her stiffened body swayed to the left. The short hairs on Jared's arm brushed momentarily against her bare, damp skin.

"It's important I fly back to Dallas tonight. I'll be bringing back something that should at least solve one of our differences."

You'll never get out of the airport in this storm, she thought. The insight Mary had given struck through his words. He's running, hiding behind his work. Anger replaced the hurt.

The great, confident, successful businessman is ducking tail and running. Confirmed bachelor, be damned. A hysterical bubble of laughter almost passed her lips. Resolutely she made her decision that, until this point, had been elusive. The only practical solution was to turn in her resignation. Selling her designs to every manufacturer in the nation was preferable to breaking her heart over Jared.

Rubbing her hand over her heart, she felt actual pain. Could the heart really break? The pain

157

was intense. A tear rolled down her cheek as she turned toward the fogged side window. *He won't make me cry,* she thought, furtively wiping the tear away.

Jaw clenched, lips drawn in a tight line, and knuckles white, Jared concentrated on driving in the storm. Elizabeth was relieved when he parked the car in front of her condo.

Not waiting for him to open the door, she fled from the car into the building. She didn't realize Jared had followed until she felt his presence behind her as she waited for the elevator. The whine of the lifting elevator cable was the single noise in the small cubicle. Elizabeth studied her feet. Muddy splashes stained her tennis shoes. The cold air from the overhead vent made the damp flesh on her arms form goose bumps. When the elevator door opened, she followed the striped carpet to the third door.

Without raising her head, she said politely, "Thank you for the picnic. Have a good flight back to Dallas." She shifted from one foot to the other while she made her polite speech.

"Elizabeth, you've misread silence as anger."

As he spoke she started to put her key into the door. Taking the key from her hand, he placed the cold metal edge against her chin and lifted it until his eyes locked with hers.

"Will you be hurt if I tell you a platonic friendship isn't enough?"

Silence.

"Neither is a hands-off policy." The key under

her chin was replaced by a curved finger. "When I get back from Dallas we'll straighten it all out." Clear green eyes searched for a response. Elizabeth controlled her features, denying him any clues.

"I don't want anything you are opposed to," he said persuasively, denying her silence. Bending down, he tenderly brushed her lips. Breaking away, he quickly strode to the elevator before he made any commitment. Elizabeth willed him to turn around and give her one more image to memorize. As he entered the elevator, he turned. Before the double doors closed, she solemnly blew him a good-bye kiss.

As if catching the kiss, his hand opened, closed, then opened, his palm over his heart.

Spending the night tossing and turning left its mark below her eyes. Dark circles were camouflaged, but not completely concealed by makeup. She felt tired as well as depressed when she walked into her office.

Removing the cover from her typewriter, she twisted a sheet of letterhead paper into the carriage. A clean, swift break would do less damage than a lingering, frustrating, dithering ending. The result would be less painful, less soul-destroying than watching a new love enter his life while she worked in the adjoining office.

Should she write a short, curt letter? Or should she come clean about how she felt? The symbols on the keyboard jumbled together as she felt the weight of tears on her lower eyelids.

Oh, hell, she thought, *I'll make it a one-liner. Typing isn't my forte.* Using the hunt-and-peck method, she typed a single line on the blank sheet of buff-colored paper. Everything but the message was professional.

"Jared enjoys songs," she muttered, pulling the sheet out and folding it twice. "Let's see how he likes this one."

Entering his darkened office, she decided to put the resignation on his desk before she let emotions rule the day and decided any pain was worth being near him. He wouldn't be in the office until Monday. She would complete the reception plans as scheduled, then peddle her designs elsewhere.

The corner of the letter tapped against the palm of her hand as though it had a life of its own. Sighing deeply, she placed it square in the middle of his desk. Since she would not be in on Monday, she wanted to make certain he saw it first thing.

The phone on her desk rang. Quickly she crossed through the connecting door and picked up the receiver.

"Elizabeth Sheffield, may I help you?" she responded automatically in businesslike tones.

"It's Mary. How's it going?"

"Fine. Can I help you with something?"

"Not really. I wanted to touch base with you. Steve called and accepted the invitation, didn't he?" Mary's usual bluntness surfaced before she could hide the reason for the call behind generalities.

"Yes, he did. In fact he seemed excited about being invited."

"Great," Mary said, sighing with relief. "Wait until you see the dress I bought yesterday. I spent the entire day shopping and making myself svelte. If this doesn't make his temperature rise, he has water in his thermometer." Mary laughed at her own joke.

Remembering the blood-boiling dress she had worn with Jared caused Elizabeth's cheeks to flame. The dress had aided in the deception and now she wished she had never seen that sexy, red, flashy gown, much less worn it to seduce Jared.

"Are you there, Elizabeth?" Mary asked when she didn't hear a responding chuckle.

"Yes. Just wool-gathering. Would you do me a favor sometime today? Go over to your parents' house and check to make certain everything but the food and flowers have arrived?"

"No problem. How's everything with you and Jared?"

Elizabeth had hoped to avoid any personal questions by changing the direction of the discussion to the reception. Guilt swept through her when she realized the letter of resignation would effect Mary's life. The marriage Mary was trying to patch up would be put to a further test if she felt obligated to return to work.

"Fine," she lied. "Are you missing work?"

Having been an active part of the business, perhaps she missed the daily routine of working.

"No way. I'm going to be a kept woman. Kept behind the sink, over the washing machine, and in the baby's room." Laughter tinkled over the phone, punctuating the word *kept*.

A kept woman was synonymous with mistress. The phrase and its meaning blared in Elizabeth's ears. A marriage license and an unborn child separated Mary from the true meaning. The phone shook in her hand. How she wished Mary's ad had asked for a wife instead of a mistress!

"Listen, Mary, I have to run. See you Saturday."

"Your voice sounds strange. If you're rushed, I can come in and help out," she graciously offered.

The lump in Elizabeth's throat threatened to block any further conversation. "No. You take care of Junior and I'll see you tomorrow. 'Bye." She hastily hung up the receiver before Mary could ask any more questions. Let Jared explain the situation to his sister. She couldn't. Swallowing repeatedly, she brought her constricted throat under control.

An hour passed before she had time to contemplate her problems any further. The florist called. The centerpiece flowers they had discussed earlier in the week were unavailable. After a lengthy discussion, Elizabeth suggested a low centerpiece using pine cones and pink and white roses which would blend with the other decorations and reinforce the house's name. After the conversation ended, she smiled wryly. She should have ordered a funeral wreath for her own front door which would herald the death of love.

Jared strolling into her office with a wide smile tossing a golden object up and down in his right hand was the last thing she expected to see. Stopping a few paces from his desk, he dropped a trinket on her desktop.

"You're supposed to be in Dallas," she exclaimed, wondering how she could retrieve her resignation before he went into his office.

"Couldn't fly out in the storm. What do you think of it?" he asked, pointing to the piece of jewelry she had ignored.

Dark eyes honed in on the trinket. A golden unicorn, her design, lay on the blank desk.

"I had to wait for the twenty-four-hour delivery service before I came to the office." Relaxing on the corner of her desk, one leg swung back and forth. "This was the cause for my urgent trip to Dallas . . ."

Elizabeth could hear his voice excitedly telling her about a new piece of machinery which would revolutionize the jewelry business.

Fingers paralyzed by anger, she could only stare at the distasteful object. A snake six inches away would have been more welcome. The manufacturer's dream could be the Grim Reaper for goldsmiths. The personal implications were more horrifying than the abortion of her designs.

"What do you think?" she heard Jared ask from outside her personal nightmare.

"I think you're despicable," she muttered, eyes misting, blurring the brilliance of the gold.

"What?"

"I won't grovel or deny you won the bet," she said, sniffing the salty tears down the back of her throat.

"Bet? For goodness' sake, Elizabeth, you don't think—"

Blinking the tears back, she raised her hand to stop his flow of words. "There is something on your desk for you that pretty well sums up what I think."

Raking his fingers through his hair he moved off her desk, and stood, legs apart, hands on hips. "I've worked like a dog this week trying to find a compromise—"

"Compromise?" Elizabeth broken in. "The only thing around here that has been compromised is me!"

"Can you deny the beauty of the workmanship in front of you?" he demanded. "Why can't you allow everyone to afford your designs?" he drilled with exasperation.

Stay cool, Elizabeth warned her mouth. *He won the damned bet fair and square. Don't give him the satisfaction of knowing his prowess in bed won more than the right to use your designs.*

"This"—her fingers plucked the unicorn off her desk and tossed it to him—"is the best machine-made piece I've had the misfortune of seeing." Crushed ice was warmer than the tone of her voice. "Now, if you'll vacate my office, I'll get back to work."

"I can see you're too angry to discuss this rationally, but I'm going to make one thing perfectly clear. The bet had been forgotten long before you appeared in my apartment. I may have used your designs to prove my philosophy about making inexpensive jewelry available for all the people instead of an elite few, but I did not use your body to win a stupid bet." Heavy, angry steps strode to the communicating door, crossed the threshold, and vanished.

"Liar," she muttered, wishing she had said the word to his face. He could deny basing the use of her designs on winning the bet, but she knew better. He had callously used her designs and her body to accomplish his goals.

Reaching into the bottom desk drawer, she pulled out her purse and prepared to leave. "Let him mass-produce his damned reception," she muttered, shooting daggers toward his office.

Jared stood between the two offices, a small vein throbbing on his forehead, green fire melting any icy look he received. In his hand he held a single sheet of paper. Wadding the paper, he threw it into her wastebasket with such force it bounced out onto the carpet.

Marching toward her desk, he visibly tried to control his rage. His jaw worked furiously, denoting his effort to restrain himself from physical violence. When he slammed his open palms on

165

the surface of her desk, she flinched and scooted her chair back as far as she could.

"TAKE THIS JOB AND SHOVE IT!" he shouted, swinging around the desk and plucking her out of the chair.

"Get your hands off of me," she hissed weakly as her head bobbed back and forth from his shaking.

"You bitch! You were going to run out on me!"

No one had ever cursed at her. *How dare he call me that!* her mind shrieked. What had been hurt and disillusionment earlier became blinding red rage.

Jared ground his lips down with the same force his hand had used on the desktop. The inner flesh of her lower lip cut into her bottom row of teeth. The taste of blood fueled the rage building within. She pelted his shoulders with ineffectual blows of her fists. The pressure on her lips increased and the soft contours of her inner mouth were raped by his tongue. Unrestrained adrenaline pumped through her veins. Angrily she fought the sinewed arms locking her in his unwanted embrace. The closer she came to hopeless defeat, the harder she struggled.

When he pushed back the length of his arms, the rage burning with the heat of a forest fire brought her clenched fist forward, slugging Jared in the eye.

Oh, my God! What have I done? Surprise and pain etched his face as automatic reflexes took over, and she pushed him away, hard. She watched round-eyed as he fought and stumbled to regain his balance, then in slow motion sank to the carpet.

She couldn't believe she had actually struck someone with her fist. She heard, rather than saw him hit the carpet with a dull, thudding noise. Dazed, she glanced at the painful, clenched fist oozing blood from one split knuckle. She knew what temporary insanity was; she had just experienced it.

Leaning over the desk, she saw the flesh around his eye turning from red to a dark purple as it began to puff closed. Her first reaction to the situation was the urge to run, but she knew her shaking body wouldn't make it to the door, much less to her car. Wobbling, she collapsed into the desk chair. Anger fled as quickly as it had consumed her. A weakness invaded her limbs as her arms hung limply over the chair.

One large tanned hand appeared as Jared used the desk to lever himself back to his feet. The violence was gone from his eyes. They were blank, devoid of emotion.

"I told you not to touch me," she said weakly.

A bemused expression crossed Jared's face. "So you did," he said as he touched the tender place below his eye. "I was slapped by a girl when I was twelve, but I've never been punched out by a man or a woman. You pack quite a wallop."

Pushing herself to her feet, Elizabeth looked closely at his swollen multicolored eye. "It just happened. I've never hit anybody in my life."

Lifting her chin, she added with false bravado, "I won't apologize. You deserved it."

His one good eye narrowed as he replied, "Then I won't apologize either. You deserved a shaking for your flippant resignation."

"You weren't supposed to see it until Monday. Why did you have to come in today before I could slink quietly into the sunset?"

"Unless my name was scraped off the door in my absence, I work here." A lopsided smile changed to a grimace when he tenderly touched his eye. "I won't accept your resignation until after Saturday."

"I planned on finishing what I started until you arrived on the scene today," she retorted with indignation.

"That you will, my dear. That you will," he threatened ominously. "Right now you're going to the cafeteria and get a bag of ice, or a beef-steak, or whatever it is you're supposed to put on a black eye."

Thankful to be excused from his presence with no further recriminations, Elizabeth kept as far away from him as physically possible and moved toward the door.

Inwardly she was ashamed of herself for giving him a black eye. Slapping a man was one thing, but hitting him with her fist . . . that was completely unladylike. A red hand imprint would quickly fade, but a black eye would take days to heal. Where was the cool façade she had tried to erect?

168

Rushing into the cafeteria, she told the manager who she was and asked for a raw beefsteak and a bag of ice without explaining the reason for the urgent need. She certainly wasn't about to tell anyone she had given her boss a knuckle sandwich.

With raw meat in one hand and a plastic bag filled with ice in the other, she entered his office. Jared lay prone of the sofa lining one wall. He emitted a growl rather than a thank-you when he took the items from her hand.

"You're welcome," Elizabeth said, flaunting his bad manners.

"Thank you for the black eye," he retorted, draping the steak over the injury. "Put the ice on your knuckles. They're probably swollen too."

They were swollen and red. She sucked in a deep breath as the cold ice added rather than detracted from the pain.

Panic, a delayed reaction, swept through her. "If you don't need me for anything else, I'll finish up my work in my own office." The need to escape had resurfaced.

"Oh, I *need* you, but at the moment I'm incapacitated." A thin veil of threat lurked in his tone of voice. "This meat doesn't help a bit." Straightening himself into a sitting position, he asked in a smooth, honeyed voice, "Want to kiss it better? I recall your offering to kiss a self-inflicted injury when I called from Dallas."

She couldn't be certain, but she thought she saw a twinkle in the eye that wasn't swollen shut.

"No? Well, give me the ice pack. I need it worse than you do." A smile definitely passed over his lips.

Passing the ice, she asked, "Truce?"

"You'd better believe it. The next time I get the urge to throttle you, I'll go out on the freeway and dodge eighteen-wheelers. It'll be safer." The low chuckle he let escape as he said the words was music to her ears. "I'm going to sneak out of here in a few minutes. Want to come with me and play nurse?"

What cat and mouse game is he playing now? She wondered. *Drat the man. Even with a black eye he is still the most attractive, adorable man I've ever seen.* She fought the urge to cradle his head rather than flee.

"Florence Nightingale I'm not," she replied, turning toward the communicating door.

With the swiftness of a panther, Jared was off the sofa, blocking the door.

"Be there Saturday," he commanded rather than asked.

Glancing over his shoulder, Elizabeth contemplated escaping out the front door.

"Don't try it," he said, reading her thoughts. "You know I always get what I go after."

He wasn't going to let her out of the office unless she capitulated. She had to accept that fact. "I'll be there." *Long enough to smile and leave,* she mentally tacked on.

"Here," he said, extending the ice pack back to her. "You have a fat lip."

Touching her tongue to the inner tissue of her mouth, she could feel its thickness.

"For that, I am deeply sorry." A sardonic grin destroyed the apology. "We'll make a gruesome twosome tomorrow. Black eye. Fat lip. Busted knuckles." His long fingers gently stroked the abrasion on her hand.

Ice water dripping from the corner of the bag splashing the top of her open-toed shoe broke the spell his nearness had begun to weave. Jerking the bag from his fingers, and with as much dignity as she could muster, she whirled out of the room.

CHAPTER TEN

Time was running out. Elizabeth reached for the small oval button that would announce her presence to the occupants of Pinerose. With any luck at all, the doorbell would be inoperative, allowing her to turn tail and flee. Any flimsy excuse would do at this point.

Coward, she berated herself. Grimacing at the grazed knuckles, she retracted her finger, running both hands around the neckline of her gown, adjusting the perfect foil for her slender beauty. It was the same chic, silky black evening dress she had considered wearing earlier in the week. Glancing over her shoulder, she looked for the metaphorical yellow stripe down her back. Only a pink silk rose nestled demurely at the waist below the plunging back was visible.

According to plan, she arrived after the reception had begun. Cars lined the drive leading to Pinerose. Safety in numbers, she had thought. If Jared's attitude about his black eye had changed from bemusement to revenge, she would be safely surrounded by his parents and their friends.

"Hell's bells," she muttered, "get it over with!" Without ringing the bell, she straightened her shoulders to military stiffness and entered the tiled hallway. The snapping and unsnapping of the gold clasp on her beaded evening bag betrayed her inner agitation.

She searched for a tall, dark-haired, lithe figure sporting a black eye. Wind whooshed from her lungs when she did not see him. The execution was delayed.

Mary, wearing a striking pink dress which complimented her dark coloring, stood by the sofa talking to an older couple. The blond man beside her was having great difficulty keeping his eyes off the cleavage exposed. As if sensing the arrival of a guest, Mary glanced up.

"Elizabeth! Come meet my family."

An older version of Jared rose from the sofa, holding both hands out in welcome.

Heart pounding, knees shaking, Elizabeth left the safety of the foyer and advanced into the flower-bedecked room. Mr. McKnight met her halfway, clasping both of her hands in the dry warmth of his own.

"You're too little to be a prizefighter," he teased.

They all know. She shuddered at the thought.

Perceptive of her discomfort, he added softly, "Jared doesn't make explanations when he doesn't want to."

She felt an immediate rapport when he squeezed her fingers before releasing them. Mrs. McKnight clasped her injured hand and introduced herself. The smile passing between husband and wife brought a guilty flush to Elizabeth's cheeks. Her conscience was flashing in neon bright letters: I HIT HIM.

"I'd like you to meet Steve, my husband," Mary said, proudly introducing the well-dressed, blond-haired, blue-eyed man who stepped from behind the sofa. The twinkle in his eye indicated he had read her unintentional message. Before releasing her hand, he pointedly brushed his thumb over her skinned knuckles.

"I've wanted to do that for years," he said with a wide grin.

The whole family knew the truth. Her mind was boggled trying to accept the fact that no one was angry. The ridicule she had feared was nonexistent. The censorous looks she had expected didn't appear. For the first time in twenty-four hours she felt as though she could make it through the afternoon without totally breaking into brittle fragments. She had cleared the first hurdle unscathed.

"You've done an excellent job of planning the reception," Mrs. McKnight praised her. "The house, the flowers, the refreshments, are all lovely. Thank you, Elizabeth."

"Can I get you something to drink?" Steve solicitiously asked.

"Thanks. Something tall, cool, and preferably nonalcoholic." *I'll need my wits about me to circumvent Jared.*

"While you're getting the liquid refreshment, I'll introduce Elizabeth to our friends," Jared's father said as he hooked her wrist through the crook of his arm.

Elizabeth circulated, meeting numerous elegantly clad men and women. Each step could lead her closer to Jared. Shifting her gaze, she searched each corner, each chair, each cluster of people for the victim of her unlucky blow. Making every effort to remember names and faces did not detract from the fear of retribution. She knew Jared was capable of evening the scoreboard with one decisive, nonphysical blow.

Nearing the back windows, she spotted him standing casually on the patio talking to George, Sara and Mr. No-Sense-of-Humor Crosby.

The dark, tailored summerweight suit emphasized Jared's height, strength, and dark coloring. Her heart constricted when George and Sara laughed at a comment he made. When her father pointed to the window, Jared pivoted, impaling her with one bright eye. A black patch covered the other.

The combination of dark hair, eye patch, and deep tan, along with the sparkling blue pool behind him, reminded her of the Errol Flynn pirate movies she had enjoyed as a child. He was a pirate. Hadn't he stolen her heart and her designs?

She pulled forcefully, trying to free her hand from the crook of Mr. McKnight's arm when she saw Jared excuse himself to enter the patio doors. Pleading eloquently with dark eyes, she begged for release. His arm stiffened like the jaws of a trap on wounded prey, refusing the plea.

"Son," the older man greeted him as the door slid open, sucking the air-conditioned coolness out of the dinette area. "Look what I've captured." Deliberately he placed her hand in his son's. "Take care of your fiancée, will you?"

Fiancée?

Bewildered, Elizabeth quickly searched Jared's nodding head for an answer. The wide grin and gleaming white teeth held no answer.

"Later," he murmured before possessively sliding his hand down her bare back, guiding her out the patio doors.

"What have you told these people?" she whispered furiously.

"Later, I said," was his curt reply as he steered her toward her father and friends. Elizabeth balked. "Later" would be too late. Ignoring her resistance, he pressed more firmly against her lower back, propelling her forward.

"Rocky," George joked referring to the boxing film, "we've been waiting for you."

A quelling look passed from daughter to father.

"Congratulations," Sara said, hugging and giggling at the same time.

One finely penciled eyebrow jerked upward, silently questioning her new fiancé. Denial hovered on her lips. Taking her hand, Jared squeezed it hard. Dangerously his eye warned that denial would bring retribution of another sort.

Jared had publicly decreed her punishment. For one black eye the forfeit was a fake engagement. The pain in her fingers didn't compare to that encircling her heart. Her eyes flashed volumes to Jared. *How would you like to have a matching set of black eyes?* He shrugged his shoulders nonchalantly. He had read the message, but was unconcerned by the threat.

The news spread like wildfire. Soon couples were approaching the newly engaged couple, offering congratulations. Gritting her teeth, she kept a stiff, frozen smile in place.

Jokes about Jared being blinded by love circulated in the outdoor area. Suavely he laughed and told the group surrounding them he had entered the battle with both eyes open. She made several false attempts to get away from him, but none were successful. His powerful arm, casually draped over her shoulder, prevented any such action.

"Would you excuse me, Jared?" Elizabeth sweetly requested. "I have to make a trip to the sandbox," she whispered close to his ear. Surely he couldn't deny that request.

"I wondered how long it would take you to think of that one. Cross your legs. You're not going anywhere without me."

Shocked at his reply, she twisted her shoulders, attempting to remove his arm. His hand stroked her upper arms as he drew her closer to his length.

Silently she wondered how far he planned on taking his revenge. The engagement had been made publicly; did the punishment end with publicly jilting her? The punishment was too severe for the crime.

Jared should never have shaken her as he did, or cursed her. She avoided remembering the actions precipitating violence on both their parts. He deserved getting poked in the eye. Didn't he? Even when she felt the punishment was cruel and unusual, she couldn't rationally justify hitting him.

A small sigh slipped through her lips as a bright idea flashed through her brain. "Jared, love, shouldn't I be wearing a ring before you introduce me as your fiancée?"

Taking a small green velvet box from his jacket, Jared countered, "I know we planned to do this together Friday, but since I had to make an unexpected trip to the Medical Center about my eye, I detoured by your dad's jewelry store and made the choice myself."

Elizabeth had sprung the trap shut with her own mouth. Cushioned on a bed of white satin, a large single diamond, mounted in a Tiffany setting, winked up at Elizabeth. With great care Jared took the engagement ring and slipped it on her finger.

A feather could have knocked her flat on the concrete. Her mouth closed, then opened again, like a fish gasping for breath. Did everyone know what was going on but fishface? Did he really plan on getting married? The ring was real. It burned her finger, branding her.

Speechless, she searched for the truth in his eye. The gleam was there. What did it mean? Could it possibly be love? She closed her mouth and shook her head.

With great tenderness Jared folded her into his arms. Lowering his head he whispered for her ears only, "I love you, Elizabeth."

He loved her; he wanted to marry her. The thoughts spun round and round in her head, making her dizzy. She felt as though a magical genie had granted her most treasured wish. Backing away, she held the ring up to her eyes. The brilliance of the diamond glittered as brightly as the single tear that slid down her cheek.

"Oh, Jared! It's beautiful."

"Well, he did have a little help," George said, puffing his chest out as only a proud father can. "I gave him a family discount."

"That's true," Jared affirmed, "but he immediately began asking about the cost of producing traditional lines using the new equipment. I won't be allowed to use my wife's designs, so I'll have to be satisfied using her father's."

179

The reception became more festive as large platters of seafood were placed on the banquet tables. Roses and pine cones, intricately woven between the dishes, were highlighted when the silver candelabra were lit. This signaled the caterer's readiness for serving the guests.

Mr. and Mrs. McKnight entered the patio area with several couples following. Mary and Steve were close behind, but their interest lay in each other rather than in food or friends.

Jared's mother cocked her head and cast him an inquiring look. The A-okay signal was flashed with his left hand before he raised Elizabeth's, displaying the diamond. Mrs. McKnight silently brought her hands together to applaud his success.

Mr. McKnight cleared his throat loudly and asked for everyone's attention.

"Friends," he began, "my wife and I are deeply touched by this gathering. I won't bore you with a sentimental speech about myself and Gems Unlimited. Just let me thank you for coming and reassure you the man taking my place may have a black eye, but his heart is as pure as gold." Mr. McKnight gestured toward Jared. "Son . . . Elizabeth." A round of applause sprinkled through the crowd. With each step closer to his father, the sound increased.

One arm looped casually over Elizabeth's shoulders, Jared took her into the center of the group. Expectantly the crowd waited for his words.

"The patch," Jared began as he touched his covered eye, "has caused more speculation tonight than the New York Stock Exchange has received in months. Not to mention the cute comments." Family and friends laughed and hooted.

"Blind as a bat; hindsight's better than foresight; blind in one eye and can't see out of the other . . . I've heard all of these and more." Chuckles became open mirth. "Blinded by love is the most accurate," he said with a chuckle, winking at Elizabeth. She caught the double meaning in his phrase and acknowledged their secret with a wide smile. "Ladies and gentlemen," Jared continued, "meet the future Mrs. McKnight . . . Elizabeth Sheffield."

A barrage of guests congratulated and shook Jared's hand. Affably he joked and received more good-natured taunts about his black eye. What would have been a humiliation for most men, Jared wore as proudly as a badge of courage. Everyone was laughing with him, not at him.

"Time to go," Jared said huskily, clasping Elizabeth's elbow and guiding her toward the door.

Without another word, only a farewell wave to both families, he guided her through the side yard, under the tall pine trees, to his car parked by the garage. Jared whistled happily. The unqualified success of the evening made both of their spirits soar. Caught by the magic of his words, she would happily have followed him to the gates of hell.

181

Before opening the car door, Jared pulled off the patch and stuck it into his jacket pocket. His eye was no longer swollen, but the deep purple bruise under it accented the smoky green coloring of the iris.

Elizabeth allowed her love to glow through her eyes, the porthole to her soul. Slowly his head lowered, and tentatively he nibbled her lips, tasting their sweetness. With a shyness they both understood, her arms crept around his neck. Jared pressed her softness between the metal of the car and himself. The tip of her tongue timidly flicked over his lips.

"Elizabeth, my sweet Elizabeth," he groaned, drawing her even closer. "Say you'll marry me . . . willingly. I want you to be my wife."

His lips brushed across her delicately fragranced shoulders. The warmth of his breath ignited the kindled fires. There could be only one answer.

"Yes, Jared. I'll marry you."

He kissed her then, claiming the sweet lips of his fiancée. She parted them, beckoning the passion to deepen. His hand, at the small of her back, covering the silk petals of the gown's only ornamentation, crushed her forward against his hips.

Her hold tightened around the strong column of his neck, letting his strength support her. The pressure of their joined lips increased as her fingers stroked and nestled in the short dark hairs

182

above his collar. Blood pounded in her veins as she felt his heart drumming against her breasts.

The masculine scent, the taste of his lips, the warmth of his body, swept away any thought other than the physical intimacy of being passionately, ecstatically kissed by the man she loved. Sweetly he tormented her when he retracted his tongue and spread moist kisses over her cheek, forehead, and ear. The hot moistness of the tip circled a tantalizing path around her ear.

"Elizabeth, you've driven me crazy all week," he said, breathing raggedly.

"Touch me," she pleaded, the tautness of her breasts aching.

"Where?"

"Anywhere! Everywhere!" Arching, she pressed her swollen breasts against him. Above all else she wanted to make love in the darkness of the pines, with the aroma of roses and his masculine scent drowning her senses.

One hand ran the length of her, from shoulder to base of spine. He whispered closely in her ear, "Say it. Tell me."

Eyes glazed with passion, lips trembling and swollen, she spoke the words he begged to hear.

"I want you. I need you. I love you."

Jared swung her around, raising her high. Whooping with laughter he sang loudly, "And three out of three ain't bad."

Feminine laughter intermingled with the deeper, huskier, male tones. The uncensored truth, spoken without reservation, was the key that would unlock future happiness. No deceit. No lies. The mask of even an innocent deception had been stripped away.

"You're making me dizzy. Put me down," Elizabeth laughingly complained, tossing her head back.

Immediately her feet touched the needle-strewn ground.

"Can I interest you in taking a gambling trip to Las Vegas?"

"Are the odds going to be in my favor?" she parried.

"You definitely will win a prize," he retorted, tucking his thumbs under the lapels of his jacket in a proud stance. "Me."

"Is that a promise?" she asked in the same lighthearted teasing voice she was hearing.

"It is."

And was.

LOOK FOR NEXT MONTH'S
CANDLELIGHT ECSTASY ROMANCES ®

Candlelight Ecstasy Romances

A woman's place—the parlor, not the concert stage! But radiant Diana Ballantyne, pianist extraordinaire, had one year before she would bow to her father's wishes, return to England and marry. She had given her word, yet the moment she met the brilliant Maestro, Baron Lukas von Korda, her fate was sealed. He touched her soul with music, kissed her lips with fire, filled her with unnameable desire. One minute warm and passionate, the next aloof, he mystified her, tantalized her. She longed for artistic triumph, ached for surrender, her passions ignited by Vienna dreams.

$3.50

Vienna Dreams

by JANETTE RADCLIFFE

Journey across 19th century Europe with lovers whose deepest passions are ignited, whose loftiest destinies are fulfilled.

The Heiress Series

Roberta Gellis

- ☐ THE ENGLISH HEIRESS, #1 $2.50
- ☐ THE CORNISH HEIRESS, #2 $3.50
- ☐ THE KENT HEIRESS, #3 $3.50

SWEET WILD WIND

by Joyce Verrette

In the primeval forests of America, passion was born in the mystery of a stolen kiss.

A high-spirited beauty, daughter of the furrier to the French king, Aimee Dessaline had led a sheltered life. But on one fateful afternoon, her fate was sealed with a burning kiss. Vale's sun bronzed skin and buckskins proclaimed his Indian upbringing, but his words belied another heritage. Convinced that he was a spy, she vowed to forget him—this man they called Valjean d'Auvergne, Comte de la Tour.

But not even the glittering court at Versailles where Parisian royalty courted her favors, not even the perils of the war torn wilderness could still her impetuous heart.

A DELL BOOK   17634-4   ($3.95)

At your local bookstore or use this handy coupon for ordering:

| | DELL BOOKS | SWEET WILD WIND   17634-4 $3.95 B044E |

P.O. BOX 1000, PINE BROOK, N.J. 07058-1000

Please send me the above title. I am enclosing $ _____ [please add 75c per copy to cover postage and handling]. Send check or money order – no cash or C.O.D.s. Please allow up to 8 weeks for shipment.

Mr. Mrs. Miss _____

Address _____

City _____ State/Zip _____

She was born with a woman's passion, a warrior's destiny, and a beauty no man could resist.

Vanessa Royall

Author of *Wild Wind Westward* and *Come Faith, Come Fire*

Gyva—a beautiful half-breed cruelly banished from her tribe, she lived as an exile in the white man's alien world.
Firebrand—the legendary Chickasaw chief, he swore to defend his people against the hungry settlers. He also swore to win back Gyva. Together in the face of defeat, they will forge a brave and victorious new dream.

$3.50

At your local bookstore or use this handy coupon for ordering: